SUZANNA ANDLER, LA MUSICA
& L'AMANTE ANGLAISE

PLAYSCRIPT 69

SUZANNA ANDLER, LA MUSICA & L'AMANTE ANGLAISE

Marguerite Duras

Translated by Barbara Bray

JOHN CALDER · LONDON

First published in Great Britain in 1975
by John Calder (Publishers) Ltd.
18 Brewer Street London W1R 4AS

La Musica was first published in France in 1965
by Editions Gallimard

© Editions Gallimard 1965

Suzanna Andler was first published in France in 1968
by Editions Gallimard

© Editions Gallimard 1968

These translations

© John Calder (Publishers) Ltd. 1975

ISBN 0 7145 3506 0 Casebound

Typesetting by Gilbert Composing Services, Leighton Buzzard
Printed by Whitstable Litho, Kent

CONTENTS

Suzanna Andler

SUZANNA ANDLER was first produced at the Arts Theatre, Cambridge, and then at the Aldwych Theatre, London, with the following cast:

SUZANNA ANDLER	Eileen Atkins
MICHEL CAYRE	John Stride
MONIQUE COMBES	Lynn Farleigh
RIVIERE	Stanley Lebor

ACT I

The curtain opens on a large empty living-room. One window looks out on pine trees. Two french windows, shut, with the shutters closed. Conventional furniture. Divan. Fireplace. Low armchairs. It is obviously a house by the sea. In one corner, furled beach umbrellas. Everything slightly untidy. Vases of dead flowers. Dead plants in pots. Newspapers.

One communicating door is open.

Bright sunshine outside.

Slight wind.

The sound of footsteps is heard from beyond the open door. Voices. Then voices and footsteps mingled.

Noise of shutters being opened.

The voices come nearer as the speakers approach the living-room.

SUZANNA. *(Off)* That makes how many bedrooms in all?

RIVIERE. *(Off)* Eight counting the one upstairs overlooking the terrace. That's the best one.

(Sound of shutters.)

SUZANNA. *(Off)* One room for Christine, one for Marc, one for Irene, two for us... Then Marie-Louise...and the girl...

RIVIERE. *(Off)* And the one upstairs makes eight.

(Silence.)

SUZANNA. *(Off)* Jean will stay for a fortnight. After that he'll come at the weekends. It's no distance by air and then only a short drive from Nice.

(Shutters again. Silence.)

Christine can have this room. She's the eldest.

RIVIERE. *(Off)* How old is she now?

SUZANNA. *(Off)* Seventeen. She's changed.

(Short silence.)

Yes, this will do for Christine. If friends come she

1

and Irene can share.

(Short silence.)

RIVIERE.   *(Off)* Was it a sudden decision—renting a different place?

SUZANNA.   *(Off)* Oh no...but you know...laziness. We wanted a big house...right by the sea. *(Pause)* How many years is it we've been going to Clair-Bois?

RIVIERE.   *(Off)* Eight?

SUZANNA.   *(Off)* Oh...?

(Silence. Footsteps.)

RIVIERE.   *(Off)* No...just a minute...Ten.

SUZANNA.   *(Off)* Ten years.

RIVIERE.   *(Off)* Yes.

SUZANNA.   *(Off; after a pause)* That's right. Irene was only a few months old...

(Sound of shutters.)

RIVIERE.   *(Off)* This room looks out on the hill, you see.

SUZANNA.*(Off)* Yes. Very nice.

(Silence.)

RIVIERE.   *(Off)* Some people phoned this morning to rent Clair-Bois. It didn't have to wait long.

SUZANNA.   *(Off)* So soon?

RIVIERE.   *(Off)* Yes. *(Pause)* Are you sorry now?

SUZANNA.   *(Off)* Oh no, not at all. Not at all.

(Footsteps.)

RIVIERE.   *(Off)* This room's smaller...

SUZANNA.   *(Off)* Yes.

RIVIERE.   *(Off)* ...and now you've seen them all except the one at the top.

(The footsteps come nearer.

They enter.

SUZANNA ANDLER *is about forty. Quietly elegant. Slim. Dark. Sad-looking. Slight suggestion of creole origins. Controlled, gentle, slightly oppressed. A femininity perhaps too marked for nowadays. Perfect poise.*

RIVIERE *is between forty-five and fifty. An estate-agent. But must have been something different before. Not at all ingratiating. Clever. Quite good-looking.*

RIVIERE. *(Entering)* Well?

SUZANNA. It's big...

(She looks round.)

RIVIERE. Let's open up...

(He opens the two french windows, revealing a wide terrace. And the sea.)

SUZANNA. *(Going out on the terrace)* Oh, how beautiful...

(Dazzling light. Slight mistral. Rough sea. They both stand up-stage on the terrace looking outward.)

RIVIERE. *(Pointing)* The harbour's over there, do you see? *(Pause)* The people who bought this place came three years running and then haven't been seen since. *(Pause)* She comes sometimes at Easter. He never comes at all.

(They continue looking out.)

SUZANNA. The mistral's blowing a bit.

RIVIERE. Yes. *(Pause)* I like it here in winter. It's quite deserted by September. It's part of the wilds again.

SUZANNA. Yes. *(Pause)* Clair-Bois was more sheltered.

RIVIERE. Oh yes. Here you're right in the wind. It blows from over there. *(Points)* A nuisance. But of course you have the sea.

(They come in from the terrace.)

Everyone well? Jean? The children?

SUZANNA. Fine, thanks.

(Pause. He looks at her.)

RIVIERE. You arrived here yesterday?

SUZANNA. *(Embarrassed)* Yes. *(Pause)* Why?

RIVIERE. Someone saw you coming out of the Hotel

de Paris. They notice everything in the winter. It's so dead here.

SUZANNA. *(As before)* Of course...

(Pause. She looks at the sea.)

Irene could go on the beach by herself. She's the youngest. You can see it easily from here.

RIVIERE. Yes. *(Pause)* Splendid children you've got, Madame Andler.

SUZANNA. They're very nice. *(Pause)* I've no complaint about my children...

RIVIERE. Nor about anything else, I imagine...? Jean's a charming man.

SUZANNA. Yes.

RIVIERE. *(Wishing to be agreeable)* Mind you, *he's* very lucky too. *(Affected by her presence)* There aren't many women like you.

(She laughs briefly.)

SUZANNA. Do you think so?

RIVIERE. Madame Andler...you're the sort of woman... One sees so many here...So when I say...

(Once again she gives a brief laugh.)

SUZANNA. There's nothing unusual about me, I assure you...*(Quite naturally)* I'm one of the most deceived wives in St. Tropez, did you know that?

(She laughs. He is intrigued.)

RIVIERE. I'm so sorry.

SUZANNA. Why?

RIVIERE. You know it doesn't mean anything?

SUZANNA. Of course. *(Pause)* And after all this time...

(Silence.)

Monsieur Riviere, if you don't mind I think I'll phone Jean. It's quite a lot of money. And then I'll let you know the answer this evening. About six.

RIVIERE. Certainly, Madame Andler. *(Pause)* It's funny your telling me that...

SUZANNA. *(Laughing)* Do you think so? *(Pause)* I'll

stay here for a bit. I want to look at the rooms again and work things out in case I do take it. You don't mind?

RIVIERE.   Of course not, stay as long as you like...
(Pause. He is intrigued) But won't you be cold?

SUZANNA.   Oh no... don't worry.

RIVIERE.   You wouldn't care to come to lunch with us?

SUZANNA.   No, thank you. No. *(Pause)* I promised a friend I'd go and see her. *(Pause)* I'll phone Jean and...either I'll ring you later or come in and see you. *(Pause)* Have you got the time?

RIVIERE.   *(Looking at his watch)* Twenty-five past eleven.

SUZANNA.   Thank you. *(Pause)* At about six then?

RIVIERE.   Right.

(He goes, perhaps somewhat reluctantly. SUZANNA ANDLER is left alone in the house. She doesn't take off her coat. She looks round the room again. Goes out on the terrace, looks down at the beach, comes in again. She seems happy. She opens a cupboard, finds a child's swim-suit, then a letter which she reads with a brief laugh. Then she listens. A woman is singing in the distance. Sounds of boats. Slight gusts of wind. Then silence. And the wind again. Perhaps she is a little afraid. She sits down on the divan, hesitates, then dials a number on the phone.)

Fairly long wait.

We do not hear MARIE-LOUISE's *voice on phone.*

SUZANNA.   Hallo? Marie-Louise? It's me...Is everything all right? How's Irene?

......

Is she being good? *(She smiles)*

......

Good... Listen, Marie-Louise... is Monsieur Andler there?

......

At Chantilly *(Pause)* Chantilly 39.

......

No, no need for that, it's nothing urgent...but if he should ring just ask him to call me at... wait a moment... *(She reads the number from the dial)* Saint-Tropez 282. *(Pause)* Have you got that? Right. *(Pause)* Well, give my love to Irene... and I'll be seeing you soon. *(Pause)* Hallo? Yes?

......

No, don't you worry... he's bound to ring to ask about Irene... Yes... Goodbye...

(She replaces the receiver. Looks at the time, goes out on the terrace, comes in again. She doesn't know what to do with herself. Finally she picks up a child's comic and lies down on the divan.

Blackout.

When the lights come on again, SUZANNA ANDLER is asleep, still holding the comic. There is a knock at the door. She doesn't hear.)

MICHEL CAYRE.   *(Off)* Anyone there?

(He enters. He is younger than SUZANNA. Between thirty and thirty-five. Good-looking, elegant, confident. His glance is intelligent and unsparing. There is often a certain deliberate vulgarity in his tone: sometimes anger. He is SUZANNA's lover. As he looks at her she starts and jumps up as if caught doing something wrong.)

MICHEL.   What have you been doing? It's three o'clock.

SUZANNA.   Oh...I'm sorry.

MICHEL.   Have you been asleep?

SUZANNA.   Yes.

(She runs her hand through her hair, like someone who's just woken up. Then sits down again on the divan.)

MICHEL.   You said half-past one at the hotel.

(She doesn't answer.

He sits beside her and recovers his composure.)

MICHEL.   You're tired.

SUZANNA.   Yes.

6

MICHEL. We drank a lot last night.

SUZANNA. Yes, we did.

(Silence. They look at each other.)

MICHEL. Have you taken the house?

SUZANNA. *(After a pause)* Not quite. It's expensive.

MICHEL. How much?

SUZANNA. A million old francs for August. *(Pause)* I must ask Jean if he's prepared to pay all that.

(She gets up and goes and sits somewhere else as if she were afraid.)

MICHEL. *(After a pause)* Didn't you agree on a price?

(Pause.)

SUZANNA. I forgot to mention it.

(He looks at her.)

I phoned home. He's gone away for the weekend. If he rings I've left a message for him to phone here between five and six.

MICHEL. Does he go away every weekend?

SUZANNA. No. Sometimes he stays in Paris and sleeps all day.

MICHEL. *(After a pause)* And supposing he doesn't ring?

SUZANNA. Then it'll have to wait till Monday. *(Pause)* I know it's a nuisance.

(He doesn't answer.)

(Apologetically) We could go to Cannes and come back on Monday. Let's go...if you'd like to...

MICHEL. *(After a pause)* Didn't he leave a number where you can ring him?

SUZANNA. Oh yes, probably. *(Pause)* I didn't ask. *(Pause)* But he'll ring to find out how Irene is, he always does when I'm not there.

MICHEL. *(After a pause)* You never know where he is.

SUZANNA. He goes to different places.

(Silence.

He gets up and goes over to the terrace.

He walks out on to the terrace and looks out.)

MICHEL.   Regular fortress, this place.

(She gets up and looks out of the window. She is always slightly uneasy when he adopts a certain tone.)

SUZANNA.   *(Constrained smile)* Yes... *(Pause)* The whole hill belongs to the house. All the rocks right down to the sea.

(Pause

She goes over to the fireplace, looks at herself in the mirror, touches her face.)

(Tired, plaintive) Oh... I used not to drink... It's you who...

(He comes back. He touches her face.)

MICHEL.   You look a wreck.

SUZANNA.   *(Joyfully)* I do, don't I?

MICHEL.   *(After a pause)* Not with Jean, at the beginning?

SUZANNA.   No.

(Short silence.)

MICHEL.   I went down to the harbour. Everything's shut. *(Pause)* I phoned my wife. I tried to write an article. *(He takes a piece of paper out of his pocket and reads)* 'A paradise peninsula bathed in perpetual sunlight...' etcetera etcetera. *(He crumbles it up and throws it away)* And then I started to wait for you.

(Short silence.)

SUZANNA.   What were you going to write about?

MICHEL.   Millionaires' wives who go to St. Tropez incognito to rent houses for the summer.

(Pause.)

Then I talked to someone in the hotel.

SUZANNA.   Oh.

MICHEL.   *(After a pause)* I told him about us. A stranger.

(He smiles.)

SUZANNA. I see

(Short silence. His tone suddenly grows harsh.)

MICHEL. *(A statement)* You don't want to go to Cannes.

SUZANNA. *(Eagerly)* Yes, I do...

MICHEL. You said 'We'll go if you want to'...

SUZANNA. I do want to... *(She stops)* What would we do in Cannes? *(Pause)* We could stay here.

MICHEL. It's dreary. *(Pause)* Don't you think?

(She doesn't answer.)

MICHEL. In Cannes everything stays open in the winter. *(Pause)* And there's no mistral. *(Pause)* We could go for two or three days. *(She doesn't answer)* Don't you ever go there in the winter? I thought...

SUZANNA. We used to go at Christmas.

MICHEL. Not now?

SUZANNA. He comes for a fortnight in the summer, that's all.

(Short silence.)

MICHEL. *(Trying to provoke)* We could walk in the sun. *(Pause)* Get some good food. *(Pause)* Make love. That never killed anybody as far as I...

(SUZANNA *is shocked. Pause.)*

(Laughing) Did I shock you?

SUZANNA. Yes.

MICHEL. Me too.

SUZANNA. *(After a pause)* You don't talk to the others like that, do you?

MICHEL. No need. They go to Cannes without making any bones about it.

SUZANNA. *(Gently, smiling)* Perhaps you want to put me off going?

MICHEL. *(Looking at her)* Perhaps. *(Pause)* I want you to go because you're made to, forced to—because you promised.

(His violence brings them together and they smile. The atmosphere becomes more relaxed.)

(With a movement towards her: youthfully)
Let's go. Let's get out of here.

SUZANNA. *(After a pause)* So if this is too dear I'll have to come back on Monday to look at some others.

(Short silence.)

MICHEL. *(Pause)* Take it, Suzanna. *(Pause)* People only hesitate about paying a million a month for a house if they can well afford it. *(Pause)* Do you hear?

(She thinks, but doesn't answer.)

What did Jean say?

SUZANNA. He said do as I like. *(Pause)* The thing is I don't know whether I like this place or not.

MICHEL. And is Jean going to tell you?

SUZANNA. He'll tell me it doesn't matter.

MICHEL. *(After a pause)* And supposing I told you the same thing.

SUZANNA. You'd be saying it just so that we should go.

MICHEL. *(Smiling)* True.

SUZANNA. Do *you* like it? *(Gesture indicating house)*

MICHEL. *(Laughing)* I couldn't care less. *(Correcting himself)* I don't dislike it.

SUZANNA. *(Obsessed)* Suppose *you* were renting it...

MICHEL. *(Interrupting)* Inconceivable.

SUZANNA. Yes...*(Pause: Unreasonably agitated)* And someone else has taken Clair-Bois now...

MICHEL. Clair-Bois?

SUZANNA. The place we used to go to.

(Pause.)

What do you think of it?

MICHEL. Ugly. Everything reeks of antique shops. As ugly as your flat in Paris. Look at it.

SUZANNA. You've never been to my flat in Paris.

MICHEL. No need. You all have the same kind of houses.

SUZANNA. *(After a pause)* Perhaps. *(Pause)* Sometimes one can see what you mean. *(Pause)* Are we all alike too—the women?

MICHEL. *(After a pause)* Yes.

SUZANNA. You're all alike too—for us.

(He looks at her.

Silence.)

MICHEL. Would you have phoned him in these circumstances ten years ago?

SUZANNA. *(After a pause)* No. I don't think so. *(Remembering)* I didn't phone even for things that were important. *(Pause)* But mostly we went away together for the weekend, so...

MICHEL. To Deauville?

SUZANNA. Yes.

MICHEL. He's always been a gambler.

SUZANNA. Yes, very much so. That's why we stopped going to Deauville.

MICHEL. *(After a pause)* Or eventually anywhere else?

SUZANNA. *(After an unusually long pause)* Yes.

MICHEL. For five years?

SUZANNA. *(After a pause)* Yes... Did I tell you that?

MICHEL. Well...sometimes you say five years, sometimes seven.

SUZANNA. Nearly nine. *(Pause)* Since Irene was born.

(Short silence.)

SUZANNA. Sometimes I go with him to the provinces. For two or three days. But not often.

(Pause)

(Correcting herself) When he goes to very out-of-the-way places...he's so terrified of being bored.

(He looks at her and says nothing.)

I don't understand what it is you want to know.

MICHEL. Nothing.

(Short silence. He looks at her.)

SUZANNA. *(Still on her idée fixe)* It was just laziness on my part, always going to Clair-Bois. There was no reason really except just laziness...

(Short silence.)

A friend of Riviere's saw us coming out of the Hotel de Paris yesterday.

MICHEL.   Do you mind?

SUZANNA.   *(After a pause)* I don't think there'd be any point.

MICHEL.   Everyone knew Jean was unfaithful to you. You do know that, don't you?

SUZANNA.   Strangers couldn't have known. *(Pause)* But all our friends did. *(She smiles)* No-one talked about it any more. *(Pause)* Did *you* know?

MICHEL.   Of course. I knew from the beginning. *(Pause)* He had quite a serious affair here two years ago.

SUZANNA.   Yes.

MICHEL.   Monique Combes.

SUZANNA.   Yes.

MICHEL.   A friend of yours?

SUZANNA. *(After a pause)* She used to come to the house. *(Pause)* Why?

MICHEL.   That was when I met him. *(Pause)* I thought you weren't there. Or that you were dead. Then one day someone told me the woman who was about in cafes in the evenings was his wife.

(He moves about the room.)

SUZANNA.   And then you saw me?

MICHEL.   No. *(Pause)* I saw you when we met in Paris. *(Pause)* You were walking along the street. *(Pause)* Without him.

(Silence.)

SUZANNA.   What did people say about us?

MICHEL.   *(After a pause)* They couldn't make it out.

(They look at one another. She conceals the truth. Pause.)

MICHEL.   Some people said you had lovers but kept it dark.

(She laughs a little.)

SUZANNA. And you? What did you think?

MICHEL. Nothing. *(Pause)* I was more interested in Jean than in you.

SUZANNA. *(After a pause)* And you're still very interested in him?

MICHEL. *(Smiling)* Yes. *(Pause)* In a different way now.

(Silence.)

Tell me why you didn't come to the hotel.

(No answer.)

SUZANNA. *(A complete lie)* I went to Les Canoubiers, to the boatyard.

MICHEL. *(After a pause)* Oh I see.

(He picks up the comic.)

(Very gently) What's the point of telling me you went to the boatyard when you didn't?

(He smiles)

SUZANNA. *(Struck)* Yes...I really don't...

MICHEL. *(As before)* ... If you'd been reading this comic, for example, you'd tell me?

SUZANNA. *(Sincerely doubtful)* Yes, I should think so. *(Pause)* Why not?

(He looks at her still waiting for her to answer his question.)

I went to Les Canoubiers.

(Silence.)

MICHEL. Right.

(Silence.)

SUZANNA. I let Riviere go and forgot I didn't have a car to get back in.

(He looks round the room. Walks about.

It looks as if she's going to admit having stayed there. But no.)

I wanted to see what the boat looked like in winter.

(Silence.)

MICHEL. Did you meet anyone?

SUZANNA. *(Hesitating)* No.

MICHEL. *(One last effort)* You might have gone to see that friend you mentioned?

SUZANNA. *(Slightly lightheaded)* No. *(Pause)* She might have come here, of course. She must know I'm here. Riviere must have told her. They knew each other. *(Pause)* Perhaps...*(She stops)* She lives in Les Canoubiers.

(Silence.

He looks at her. Then goes out on the terrace.

Silence.)

MICHEL. Not a soul.

(Silence.)

They say no-one sets foot here in winter. *(Pause)* And in the spring they find corpses in the houses. *(Pause)* No explanation whatever.

(He lights a cigarette.)

Have you seen all over? *(Gesture)*

SUZANNA. Yes. It's a big place. You can see over if you like.

MICHEL. No. *(Pause)* That works out at thirty-three thousand smackers a night.

SUZANNA. *(After a pause)* Jean's making a lot of money just now. At least I think so... *(She tries to pull herself together)* I'd be surprised if he didn't ring home. It would be the first time...

(He is used to her idées fixes and is thinking about something else.)

(Pursuing the bee in her bonnet) If I'd taken a liking to it straight away I'd have taken it without phoning him. *(Pause. She looks at him)* Couldn't we go somewhere else instead of Cannes?

MICHEL. *(His thoughts elsewhere)* Anywhere you like.

SUZANNA. Aix? *(Pause)* Marseilles?

(Silence. He looks at her. She doesn't look at him.)

MICHEL. *(Calling her)* Suzanna.

SUZANNA. *(Suddenly uneasy, as if woken up)* Yes.

MICHEL. *(Hiding a sudden fear)* Do you still want me?

SUZANNA. Yes. *(Pause. Then back to idée fixe)* I
ought to have come down a couple of months ago.
There's nothing left now unless you pay the earth.

(They are each deep in different preoccupations.)

(Suddenly) What's the time?

MICHEL. *(Looking at his watch)* Ten past four.

SUZANNA. What if Riviere wasn't telling the truth and
Clair-Bois is still free?

(Silence.)

MICHEL. What did I say to you the first day, the very
first evening? *(Pause)* Do you remember?

SUZANNA. Why do you ask? *(Pause, then, not waiting
for an answer)* You said, 'This is going to be just
an unimportant affair. Don't go thinking it's a
grand passion.'

(Silence.)

Had you forgotten?

(No answer.)

Do you still say that?

MICHEL. Yes.

SUZANNA. You'd had a lot to drink. It was when I
was getting ready to go.

MICHEL. *(Elsewhere. Already trying to work out the
past)* And after that you left Paris?

SUZANNA. Yes. I went to Bordeaux. It'd been
arranged a long time. *(Pause)* You phoned the day
after I got back.

MICHEL. *(Remembering)* I'd rung before while you
were still away.

SUZANNA. They didn't tell me. *(Pause)* This is the
first time we've talked about the past.

(Silence.)

Last night you said you understood how someone
could have loved me and then one day have
stopped.

MICHEL.   No. *(Pause)* I said 'have suddenly chucked you out'.

SUZANNA.   *(Smiling)* You've got a good memory for words.

MICHEL.   *(After a pause)* I've been repeating those over and over again since this morning. *(Pause)* You understand how someone might say that to you?

SUZANNA.   *(After a pause)* Yes. But no-one ever had. *(Pause)* I think I'd been waiting a long time to meet you. *(Pause)* It had to happen.

(Silence.)

The house had got to be just for the children. *(Pause)* We don't speak.

MICHEL.   My house is the same. Solid as a rock.

SUZANNA.   With the woman who went away with you for the week-end?

MICHEL.   Yes. She became my wife.

SUZANNA.   She suddenly became faithful to her lover the same as she'd once been faithful to her husband.

MICHEL.   That's right. *(Pause)* A millstone.

SUZANNA.   *(Smiling)* Yes.

(Silence.)

It's because of you I've given up Clair-Bois I think. So that we can have a place of our own for a fortnight this summer.

MICHEL.   You know it'll end this summer?

SUZANNA.   Perhaps. *(Pause)* Not now.

MICHEL.   Now what?

SUZANNA.   *(Surprised at the question)* Now I'm taking this place?

(He doesn't react to this bizarre idea.)

(Pause) I thought of not coming back to St. Tropez at all. But the children have their friends here, they wouldn't be happy anywhere else. *(Pause)* Sailing past Les Colonnades I used to say I'd spend a summer here one day.

(He is silent. She goes on slowly.)

We used to say the same thing about other houses

too. *(She has slipped unconsciously into 'we')* 'It would be nice to have an affair there; a new love.' *(Pause)* It was a sort of game.

MICHEL. *(Struck)* Did you talk to him about renting Les Colonnades?

SUZANNA. No. Oh, he agreed to make a change, the actual house was neither here nor there.

MICHEL. *(Narrowly)* Did he mention it first or did you?

SUZANNA. I did.

MICHEL. Are you sure?

SUZANNA. Yes... it was all exactly the same to him. He's never in in the summer. He just comes home to sleep, that's all.

(Silence.)

MICHEL. *(Looking at her)* It was something he could do for you—rent the house because you liked it.

SUZANNA. *(After a pause)* Yes. *(Pause)* He's very attached to me.

(Silence. In a different tone, lower.)

MICHEL. You won't ever leave him.

SUZANNA. Perhaps. *(Pause)* Yes, perhaps I might.

MICHEL. He won't leave you either. *(Pause)* Though that's not so certain.

SUZANNA. He'll never leave me as long as I'm alone. *(Pause. Gently)* I'm not in his way.

MICHEL. Are you alone now, Suzanna?

SUZANNA. *(After a pause)* I think so.

MICHEL. Will you know—when you're not alone any more?

SUZANNA. *(A flash of sincerity)* He'll know for me. *(Pause)* I know about him when... *(Pause)* Sometimes he goes away for several weeks. Every time he says there's a possibility he may not come back.

MICHEL. *(After a pause)* And you believe him.

SUZANNA. *(After a pause)* I believe what he says.

MICHEL. You wait.

SUZANNA. I'm used to it.

MICHEL. He's used to it too, I suppose?

SUZANNA. No. He forgets me while he's away, so he's always... amazed to find me there. Do you see? It's only natural. Yes. *(Pause)* It's made a great difference. *(She smiles)*

MICHEL. As big as all that?

(Silence.)

SUZANNA. It was the first time I'd been unfaithful to Jean.

(He puts his head in his hands.

Silence.)

MICHEL. You were telling the truth just then. How strange.

(Silence. He doesn't speak.)

SUZANNA. I don't think it occurred to me. *(Pause)* It didn't occur to anyone else either. *(Pause)* Some women make men think of marriage rather than...love. *(Longer pause)* It's a long time ago. I really couldn't say why... really... I don't know...

(He is silent. He gazes at her fixedly.)

(Smiling) You'd said don't let's talk about the past. *(Pause. Brief laugh)* That I had to be prepared for it to end at any time, between one meeting and the next. *(Pause)* One's nervous about saying a thing like that. I was afraid you might be repelled...or scared...

(He still doesn't say anything.)

One forgets straight away... in an hour I'd forgotten.

(Long silence.

He stays there without speaking.)

Sometimes Jean could see I was lonely, so... *(Pause)* *I* used to ask *him*.

(He smiles, and lets her go on.)

It was hard to endure sometimes...especially in summer when all the other people...

(She stops. Afraid.

18

MICHEL *stares at her.)*

MICHEL.   But... tell me... did Jean *want* you to be
unfaithful to him?

SUZANNA.   *(After a pause)* He said I ought to. *(Pause)*
I left it long enough.

(MICHEL is silent. Gradually gets frightened.)

He believes in that sort of thing. A lot of people
do. You do, don't you?

MICHEL.   So you told him?

SUZANNA.   *(After a pause)* No.

MICHEL.   *(Still gently, trying to trap her)* But if that
was what he wanted? What had been decided on?

SUZANNA. *(Gestures 'No'.)*

MICHEL.   Why?

(Silence. She doesn't answer.

He smiles.)

You lied to us both then.

SUZANNA.   *(With a cry)* I don't understand...

MICHEL.   No.

(Silence.)

SUZANNA.   What is there to be sorry about?

MICHEL.   Nothing.

(He is abstracted for a moment. Silence.

He comes over to her.)

Have you ever thought of leaving me, Suzanna?
(She gestures 'No'.) Not once? *(She gestures as
before.)* For an hour? *(As before.)* The first day?

SUZANNA.   No.

*(He is shattered. She gives him a hostile look, for
the first time.)*

No.

(She goes on looking at him without answering.)

MICHEL.   *(Smiling)* Perhaps we've both lost you.
(Pause) Jean and me.

SUZANNA. *(Violently)* You deliberately ask me questions

I can't answer. *(Pause)*

(No answer.

He goes towards the door.)

(Almost screaming) Where are you going?

MICHEL. I'll wait for you in the room. It's half-past four. I'll be there till half-past six, till after the phone-call.

SUZANNA. *(Still uncertain)* Perhaps I could ring Paris? Ask for his number? Ring him? Why not? We could call in at Riviere's office and then leave, we could be in Cannes in time for dinner?

(Silence.)

MICHEL. No. You won't do it.

SUZANNA. *(Frightened)* Where will you be after half-past six?

(He doesn't answer.)

You don't know?

MICHEL. No.

(He goes out.

She is left alone. She stands there without moving. Picks up the telephone, puts it down again. Gradually she forgets MICHEL CAYRE. *She opens cupboard doors, looks inside, takes things out and puts them back again, apparently without getting any pleasure out of it. She sits down. Remains quite still for a long time. Then goes out.)*

END OF ACT I

ACT II

*Out of doors. The boatyard, or the grounds of Les
Colonnades down by the sea, or the beach itself, a
bare stretch like a dune. In any case, some place
that's deserted.*

SUZANNA ANDLER *and* MONIQUE COMBES *are
standing there. They have only just come.* MONIQUE
is a shade younger than SUZANNA. *They are looking
towards the house; i.e. towards the auditorium.*

SUZANNA.   We wanted to make a change.

MONIQUE.   *(Still looking towards the house)* I've never
been inside.

SUZANNA.   *(Not looking at it any more)* It's big,
that's all.

MONIQUE.   Expensive, I suppose?

SUZANNA.   A million and a half for August.

MONIQUE.   *(Looking at her doubtfully)* Good heavens.

SUZANNA.   *(Using* MICHEL's *words)* It works out at
thirty-three thousand smackers a night.

MONIQUE.   *(Smiling)* Yes.

(Constrained silence.)

How are you, Suzanna? And Jean? And the
children?

SUZANNA.   Very well.

MONIQUE.   How long are you here for?

SUZANNA.   I leave again this evening.

(MONIQUE affects surprise.)

MONIQUE.   So soon?

SUZANNA.   I'm going to Cannes.

*(MONIQUE strolls about a bit and looks round
admiringly.*

MONIQUE.   It's a beautiful spot.

SUZANNA.   Quiet. It must be rather depressing in the
evening.

MONIQUE.   The evening? Oh, it's like that all along the

21

coast. Are you going to take it?

SUZANNA. I'm expecting Jean to ring between five and six. *(Pause)* If he agrees I'll take it.

(SUZANNA *looks towards the house and is silent.)*

MONIQUE. I was only passing. I don't want to bother you.

SUZANNA. You're not bothering me...on the contrary. *(Pause)* I was on my way here when I met you. I was going to see the boat.

MONIQUE. I come here myself sometimes. *(Pause)* Jean phoned me the day before yesterday. I knew you were coming today.

SUZANNA. I see.

MONIQUE. He asked me to help you decide if you were torn between several places.

*(*MONIQUE *smiles.*

They avoid looking at each other.)

SUZANNA. No need. It was Les Colonnades I wanted. *(Pause)* To see inside.

(Silence.)

MONIQUE. *(After a pause)* You were seen with someone in the harbour yesterday evening ... *(She smiles awkwardly)* ... someone not Jean Andler.

SUZANNA. Who saw me?

MONIQUE. Oh... a shop-keeper.

(Silence.)

Do I know him?

SUZANNA. I don't think his name would mean anything to you. He's a journalist who writes for awful rags...that you never set eyes on.

(Silence.

MONIQUE *thinks she understands. And tries to hide it.)*

MONIQUE. *(Quite naturally)* You're at the Hotel de Paris?

SUZANNA. Yes.

(Silence.)

MONQIUE. How long has it been going on?

SUZANNA. Seven or eight months...about.

(She sits down on the sand or against part of the dock.)

MONIQUE. Would you have come to see me?

SUZANNA. *(After a pause)* I'd have tried to call at your place before I met him.

MONIQUE. Couldn't you have brought him?

SUZANNA. *(Quickly)* Oh no... Why? *(Pause)* Did Jean say anything to you?

MONIQUE. *(Lying)* Oh no.

(SUZANNA *looks at her and looks away again.)*

Does he know?

SUZANNA. No.

(Short silence.)

MONIQUE. Are you sure?

SUZANNA. *(After a pause)* Yes.

(She is the only person who could say this.)

MONIQUE. *(Change of tone: smiling, gentle)* I can't bring myself to believe it, Suzanna...

SUZANNA. *(A brief laugh. Looking away)* It's true all the same.

(Silence.)

MONIQUE. Haven't you and Jean ever talked about the possibility?

SUZANNA.*(After a pause)* But not since... not for some time...

MONIQUE. Exactly... That's because he knows...or because he suspects something.

SUZANNA. No. He can only find out for certain from me. *(Pause)* I don't know how it will be. *(Pause)* We'll see.

(Silence.)

Has the work been going well this winter?

MONIQUE. I've fitted out a nursery school at Juan-les-Pins.

23

SUZANNA.   That's fine. *(Pause)* Haven't you been to Paris?

MONIQUE.   I was there for a couple of days in October—someone drove me up. You weren't there. You were in Bordeaux, I think.

(Short silence.)

SUZANNA.   I go with him sometimes when he's reporting on something. It's amusing.

MONIQUE.   What do you tell Jean?

SUZANNA.   Oh, nothing...why should he care? On the contrary...

MONQUE.   Yes.

(SUZANNA looks at her and at once looks away again.)

SUZANNA.   Sometimes Jean and I go away together too. But not often. Only when he's afraid he might get bored. You know how he dreads being bored.

(MONIQUE didn't know about these trips.)

MONIQUE.   I see.

(Silence.)

SUZANNA.   Do you think he'll be pleased about what's happening to me?

MONIQUE.   *(After a pause: her reply is calculated and conventional)* Deep down I think he'll be happy about it. But one can never tell beforehand... At first I think he'll suffer. *(Pause)* What do you think?

SUZANNA. *(Return to sincerity)* He'll suffer a bit. *(Pause)* He's been entirely free for a long time... Irene must have been four...and she's ten now. *(Pause)* Six years.

MONIQUE.   *(After a pause)* He's talked to me about it once or twice. *(Pause: lightly)* You know he and I are good friends...

SUZANNA.   I know. *(Pause)* I didn't know he talked about it.

MONIQUE. *(Softening the blow)* Oh...just out sailing... only in passing.

(Silence.)

SUZANNA.   Did he tell you there'd been nothing between us for six years?

MONIQUE.   *(After a pause)* Nothing as specific as that. *(Pause)* It was just that I understood...

(In fact MONIQUE *never really knew what the situation was.)*

SUZANNA.   At least... He could see I hadn't got anyone...so sometimes, you see...

(Short silence. MONIQUE *pays close attention.)*

It was *I* who asked *him. (Pause: it's as if she were slightly drunk)* Not always. *(Pause)* But it came to the same thing. He could see it was sometimes difficult to bear. In the summer there'd be nothing but that everywhere... *(more quickly, suddenly)* He had all the women he wanted. I was always with the children. *(Pause: she smiles)* In the end I'd become unapproachable to anyone except him...

(Silence, She comes back to MICHEL CAYRE.)

He's married. With two children. He could do something better than what he's doing. He's clever, I think. He says he's a Communist. That's what they all say. Who knows? He's mainly interested in making money. *(Pause)*

MONIQUE.   *(Pause)*   You look pretty.

SUZANNA.   No. *(Pause)* Far from it. *(Pause)* I'd almost stopped being a woman, belonging to one man like that...I'd become...

MONIQUE.   *(Forced laugh)* What?

SUZANNA.   *(With a grimace)* A sort of elderly girl.

MONIQUE.   No.

(Silence.)

SUZANNA.   *(Not answering: suddenly conventional)* Being a woman means having different experiences?

MONIQUE.   *(Pause)* Or just one, perhaps. A thousand in one. *(Pause)* Jean wanted it.

SUZANNA.   Yes. *(Pause)* He used to say, 'I wish you'd... *(She stops)* One can't repeat things like that.

(Silence.

They don't look at each other.)

MONIQUE.   He wanted it to happen...

25

SUZANNA. *(Painfully)* Sometimes. *(Pause)* Do you understand?

MONIQUE. *(With a violence she can't wholly restrain)* Not really. Mine are always short-term affairs. I don't know the sort of thing that may happen between people in the long term.

(Silence.)

SUZANNA. *(With animation)* At first this autumn, he wanted to live with me straight away. It's funny. *(Pause)* I make men want to live with me.

*(*MONIQUE *is silent, struck by this.)*

When I was young they used to propose to me straight away. *(Pause)* Jean as well.

(She smiles.)

MONIQUE. *(After a pause)* He says you inspire sensible feelings. *(Pause)* At first. *(Pause)* And then it changes... changes completely.

SUZANNA. *(Trying to hide her surprise)* Dear me.

MONIQUE. I couldn't quite understand what he really meant that day. He said you were... wait a minute... he used some long word... unknowable—yes, that's it—*(Pause)* except through desire.

*(*SUZANNA *doesn't answer.)*

(After a pause: slowly) You must understand what he meant.

SUZANNA. *(Still insincerely)* No, not very well.

*(*MONIQUE *smiles faintly, trying to conceal her pain.)*

SUZANNA. *(Animated) He* wants all the women too. He's not faithful to me. I don't mind at all. *(Pause)* You see, Jean... *(Pause)* He's witty. Amusing. Spiteful. Yes, spiteful.

MONIQUE. *(After a pause)* Is it serious?

SUZANNA. *(After a pause: Completely sincere)* Perhaps.

(Silence.)

MONIQUE. *(After a pause)* Any question of leaving Jean for him?

SUZANNA. *(After a pause)* Not yet... but...

(Silence.)

MONIQUE. *(Painfully)* Jean won't leave you this time.

SUZANNA. *(Laughing at the idea: witty, mischievous)* Oh no! The first time! That would be too much to expect! *(Pause; serious again)* but ... who knows?

MONIQUE. *(Slightly forced smile)* People always talk about having 'lovers', in the plural.

SUZANNA. Yes. *(Pause)* But this time was very important to me.

MONIQUE. *(Delicately)* The first... isn't it?

SUZANNA. Yes.

(They look at each other. MONIQUE smiles.)

MONIQUE. It doesn't seem possible.

SUZANNA. *(After a pause)* It's just been like this day after day. *(Pause)* For seventeen years.

(MONIQUE *looks at her without answering.*)

(Lonely) They knew one another.

MONIQUE. *(Affecting surprise)* Really?

SUZANNA. They used to see each other in the evenings when we were here. They've been sailing together.

MONIQUE. I know him, then?

SUZANNA. No. At least...It was last year. *(An allusion to the affair between* MONIQUE *and* JEAN *two years ago)* You probably know him by sight. But you can't know which one he is. *(Pause)* Nothing happened here. It was only in Paris. *(Pause)* It all took place in the traditional manner, one afternoon in a hotel. *(Pause)* Except that I didn't have to tell lies when I got home, because Jean never asks any questions. *(Pause)* I'd sworn to myself I'd be unfaithful to him.

MONIQUE. You'd promised him?

SUZANNA. *(Pause)* Yes. It was ridiculous, it couldn't go on. *(Pause)* And then, quite suddenly, we couldn't do without each other. *(Pause; she smiles)* I often drive him crazy.

MONIQUE. *(After a pause)* Perhaps you love him?

(Silence)

27

(After a pause) If you didn't love him you wouldn't try to hide it from yourself?

SUZANNA. *(Thinking)* No? Why?

MONIQUE. Would you know?

SUZANNA. I think so, wouldn't I? I got up early this morning to come here. *(Pause)* I'm very tired. We drink all night long.

MONIQUE. I didn't understand... I thought you seemed...

SUZANNA. What?

MONIQUE. Different. And at the same time... staggeringly...the same as you would have been if you'd spoken...before.

(SUZANNA *is silent.*)

What you've just said—that's not the whole truth, is it, Suzanna?

SUZANNA. *(After a pause)* Don't ask.

(Silence. They stroll about a bit. SUZANNA speaks sometimes fast, sometimes slowly, in what follows.)

(A change comes over her; she is suddenly unclouded and luminous) A fortnight after I got back from St. Tropez—here he'd hardly looked at me—like all Jean's friends... *(Slowly)* we met one evening. There was a storm. *(She remembers)* It was pouring. I was waiting outside a cafe for it to stop. He came in out of the rain. *(Remembering)* At first we were surprised, it was so sudden. *(Pause)* He took me into the cafe. We stayed an hour. *(Pause)* Then he drove me home in his car.

(Silence.)

We stopped on the quai de Passy. A metro was just going by over the Auteuil viaduct. He turned to me and said look it's beautiful. *(Pause)* Then he said: *(She recalls this slowly)* 'I suddenly want you. How strange.' *(Pause, then more quickly)* The next morning he rang and asked me to go away for the weekend the same evening.

(Silence.)

That was one Friday in September. *(Pause)* I said I'd go. *(Pause)* After lunch Jean told me he'd be going away for the weekend. He goes every weekend but he always says. I don't know where he goes. *(Pause)* Somewhere near Chantilly? *(Pause)* And perhaps here sometimes? He does sometimes go by air. (MONIQUE *does not react. Pause)* Marie-Louise was away on holiday. *(Pause)* I said, 'I'm going away for the weekend.' He didn't ask any questions. *(Pause)* Did he say he was tired of me?

MONIQUE. *(Hesitating)* Not of you. Of marriage.

SUZANNA. How did he say it?

MONIQUE. *(After a pause)* I'd like to know her some other way.

(Short silence. SUZANNA looks down.)

SUZANNA. I asked him *(Brief laugh)* if this time he could stay and look after Irene. *(She laughs)* It was the first time in seventeen years. *(She laughs)* He said yes, of course, and asked me when I'd be back. I said, 'Sunday evening.'

(She stops. Silence.)

I didn't go back on Sunday evening. *(Pause)* I went back on the Tuesday, in the afternoon. *(Pause. She remembers)* The children were still at school. *(Pause)* Jean was at the office. *(Pause)* The house was empty, *(Pause)* as if we were dead.

(Silence.)

The next week we went to Bordeaux *(Longish pause)* The weather had got warm again, I remember *(Pause)* We went right to the coast.

(Silence. MONIQUE has listened very attentively to this version of the facts.)

MONIQUE. He never spoke to me about that weekend.

SUZANNA. He'll never speak to anyone about it.

(Solitary)

MONIQUE. I don't believe it happened as you say.

SUZANNA. As you like. It's not important.

MONIQUE. No.

(Silence.)

You could tell me the truth *(Smile)* You could tell me. *(Smiling, but in pain)* I've only just passed

29

through your life, and it'll remain intact, safe from any distortion. *(Pause)* Any change. *(Pause)* And yet you lie to me too.

SUZANNA.   He never told me I lied. *(Pause)* He told me 'She's the only one who tells the truth' *(Smiles)* He smiled when he said it.

(Silence.)

MONIQUE.   I think it was through him you entered into untruth. *(Pause)* Or rather, you entered into the temple together. No one believed in your marriage any more. And yet it existed with a strength one would never suspect. That's when the lying began. *(After a pause)* I don't understand what you say.

(MONIQUE *looks at her.*)

It's even possible you don't know.

(Silence. They look at one another.)

SUZANNA.   *(Smile)* That doesn't mean you can't go on talking.

MONIQUE.   *(After a pause)* Once I saw Jean Andler watching his wife. She was swimming. She was quite a long way out and the sea was rather rough. The look escaped him. *(Pause)* No one noticed it, except me.

SUZANNA.   *(Laughing)* Always afraid something's going to happen to me ... It's ridiculous ... quite ...

MONIQUE.   *(As if there had been no interruption)* Everyone thought of Jean Andler as alone. *(Pause)* People were sorry for him: *(Smile)* women. All Jean's adventures started the same way: women were sorry for him for being misunderstood, and wanted to understand him. *(Longish pause)* Soon, after it began, they'd see Jean Andler's wife wasn't in the way. Never. *(Pause)* They forgot she existed.

(Silence.)

When Jean Andler's affairs were short they forgot his wife existed for good and all. When the affairs were long, at a certain point they'd discover in Jean Andler a sort of ... silence ... a sort of strange dimension that nothing could reach. It was as if there was a wall encircling some ultimate Jean Andler, and as if that wall were insurmountable.

(Pause) Then they'd wonder if perhaps he didn't, say, believe in God *(Smile)*, without admitting it ... or if there wasn't, deep and far inside him, a kind of inability to experience a real passion ... a kind of infirmity of feeling...

(Silence. SUZANNA listens as if it were all about someone else.)

SUZANNA.   *(Involuntarily)* That's beautiful.

(Silence.)

MONIQUE.   *(Continuing)* After a long time *(she smiles)* of lying awake at night, they'd see that perhaps the ultimate silence of Jean Andler concealed the love of a woman. *(Pause)* They'd wonder if he knew.

(Silence.)

You'll tell him this evening?

SUZANNA.   Perhaps.

(Silence.)

MONIQUE.   Will he be coming this summer?

SUZANNA.   I think so. *(Pause)* We've never talked to each other about him, have we?

MONIQUE.   *(With deliberation)* You knew.

SUZANNA.   *(After a pause)* Like everyone else. *(Pause)* No more. He never spoke to me about you.

MONIQUE.   *(After a pause)* What didn't you know?

(Short silence.)

SUZANNA.   If you'd been unhappy.

MONIQUE.   *(After a pause)* He doesn't know.

SUZANNA. *(Smiling)* You started to go sailing just to be with him.

MONIQUE.   *(Smiling)* Yes. I'd have done anything. *(Pause)* You were never worried about ... about that business, were you?

SUZANNA.   *(After a pause)* No.

(Silence. MONIQUE looks down. She and SUZANNA are both standing.)

MONIQUE.   You were right. *(Pause)* Several times I'd have liked to talk to you about it but you didn't seem to want to.

SUZANNA.   What was the point of talking to me? *(Pause)* All I could have told you was to be careful with Jean.

MONIQUE.   How?

SUZANNA.   *(Searching for the words)* He enjoys women's company so much they often think he's... singling them out. *(Pause)* But he isn't. For him it's the same as gambling. *(Pause)* You wouldn't have listened to me. When you used to go off with him—from the beach—I remember—you were crazy.

MONIQUE.   *(After a pause)* Yes. *(Pause)* It's strange you should talk to me about it today.

SUZANNA.   Everything's different now. *(Pause)* It's as if I couldn't stop talking now.

MONIQUE.   About whom?

(Silence. No answer.)

SUZANNA.   *(Slowly, as if tired)* Even when Jean's here he wants to come. So that everything should be clear. They got on quite well together before, you know. He says Jean will be pleased when he knows it's him.

MONIQUE.   *(Thinking of something else)* Who can tell? Perhaps.

(Silence.)

It'll all happen by itself. Don't think about it.

SUZANNA.   I don't. *(Pause)* Jean must have made a lot of money this year. He never says anything to me about it.

MONIQUE.   If you're thinking about the house I'm sure you needn't worry. Not in the least.

SUZANNA.   *(Looking at her)* I'm sure too. He spends all he makes, every penny. *(Pause)* It's of no importance. He never mentioned it. *(Pause)* What time do you make it?

MONIQUE.   Ten past five.

(Silence. They are both thinking.)

SUZANNA.   I'm going back to the house.

(Silence. SUZANNA is exhausted.)

MONIQUE.   There's been a man driving round St. Tropez

in a sports car all the morning. In the winter you notice everyone. Tall, fair, good-looking, blue eyes— is that him?

SUZANNA. *(Drawing back)* No.

MONIQUE. I've seen him before down here. He looks like one of the habitués to me. I think he's a journalist too. I expect he plays poker in the Cafe des Arts.

SUZANNA. No, no, that's not the one.

MONIQUE. *(After a pause)* I'm wrong, then?

SUZANNA. Yes.

(Silence.)

MONIQUE. *(Smiling)* Where does Jean go at the weekends, do you know?

SUZANNA. There are several women, I think. One of them's a model.

(Silence.)

MONIQUE. See you in the summer, then, Suzanna?

SUZANNA. See you in the summer.

(They kiss.)

MONIQUE. *(As if worried)* Won't you come down to the harbour with me?

SUZANNA. I'm waiting for Jean to phone.

MONIQUE. Of course...Don't stay too late.

SUZANNA. As soon as he's rung I'll go.

(Short silence. MONIQUE goes, and is no longer visible.)

MONIQUE. *(Off)* I was forgetting to tell you ... Do you remember Bernard Fontaine?

SUZANNA. Yes.

MONIQUE. *(Off)* He was killed in a car crash the day before yesterday.

(SUZANNA stands motionless. She doesn't answer.)

You were in love with him. *(Pause)* You didn't want to admit it but you liked him didn't you?

SUZANNA. *(After a pause. Calmly)* Perhaps. Now that he's dead. *(She corrects herself)* Or now that you say

33

so? Funny ... I dreamed about him the other night.

MONIQUE.   Will you dream of all the others now?
Goodbye, Suzanna.

SUZANNA.   Goodbye.

(She also goes off and disappears.

The stage is empty.)

MONIQUE.   *(Off. In the distance)* You already look as
if you're going home.

(No reply from SUZANNA.

Empty stage.

Silence.)

BLACKOUT

END OF ACT TWO

ACT III

The living-room of the house. Empty at first.

Then SUZANNA *enters.*

The sky is overcast now, with a few sunny intervals, four or five in all, which SUZANNA *immediately notices. It is as if she were keeping a watch on the weather.*

She looks round the room. And at the sea. Walks about, then goes and sits down some distance from the phone. She looks at it. Then does nothing but sit there. When the phone rings she doesn't get up at once. Then she springs up quickly. She answers Jean Andler in a calm voice, different from the one we know so far. We do not hear Jean's voice.

SUZANNA.   Hallo? Yes, it's me

What? *(Pause)* Oh ... sorry ...

No. It's about the house. It's expensive. A million for August. So I wanted to talk to you before I ... that's all.

(Hesitating slightly) Les Colonnades. *(Pause)* Yes. We used to sail past it... *(She stops)* When houses look so attractive from outside one's always a bit disappointed... but still...

(Silence.)

(Incapable of saying so outright) Well, in the evening... yes... perhaps the grounds *are* a bit dreary, but ...

(Silence.)

Yes, I'm there now.

It's big... eight bedrooms...and only a hundred and fifty yards from the sea. There's a little private beach that's quite safe, even Irene will be able to go there on her own. But it seems expensive to me.

(After a pause: disappointed) Right. *(Pause)* The best thing is the big terrace looking down over the rocks. *(Pause)* What's it like in Paris?

(Silence.)

(Harshly) I'm staying at the Hotel de Paris.

(He doesn't answer.)

(Aggressively) It's deserted here in the winter. As if no-one set foot here for ten years.

(Silence.)

Yes, I'm still here.

(Silence.)

Clair-Bois is already let.

No, no. *(After a pause; aggressively)* Well, I think we kept on going there too long. *(Pause)* So what shall I do?

(Annoyed) Right.

(Short silence.)

(Troubled) In two or three days. *(With great difficulty)* I'm going to Cannes for a bit first. This afternoon. I was just waiting for you to call first.

(Silence.)

(Pause, then in one breath, harshly) I'm going to see Monique. I went to her place here and they told me she's working on a nursery school in Cannes.

(Silence.)

(Her voice dropping suddenly) Yes. That's right.

(Expressionless) Actually, I met her just now at Les Canoubiers.She was on her way here.

(Pause) That's right, She's really working at Jean-les-Pins.

She told me Bernard Fontaine had been killed in a car accident. Three days ago.

(Silence.)

Monique says the same.

(Silence.)

And yet I met him once outside a cafe—it was raining, I remember. *(Pause)* And he didn't ask me to see him again.

(Silence. The tone becomes tenser.)

(After a pause) Yes.

(Suddenly completely forthright) No.

(Silence. The dialogue becomes very slow.)

Did someone tell you?

(Charged silence.)

Even if you hadn't said anything...I'd have told you today...I'd made up my mind...

(Lying) About eight months? ... Not so long, you think? ... Six?

(Silence.)

October. *(Pause)* Before you went to Bordeaux.

(Pause)

I wasn't sure you'd understand.

(Silence.)

(After a pause; completely sincere) I don't know. *(Pause)* He says it's serious.

(Silence.)

(Sudden access of feeling) I talked to Monique for a long time. *(Pause)* A long time. *(Pause)* I told a lot of lies.

No. *(Agitated again)* But about everything... everything... If she ever talks to you about what we said...

(She stops. Silence.)

I lie to him about us.

(She stops. Silence.)

Yes. I'm here.

Yes. *(Pause)* I think I'll come back to Paris.

(Silence.)

(Quite clear and straightforward) I'd like to kill myself.

(She doesn't answer.)

Yes. I'm here. No. *(Pause)* There's nothing to worry about.

(Silence.)

No. *(Pause)* It's all over. *(Pause)* It only lasted a moment. *(Pause)* You understand.

(Silence.)

No. *(Pause)* I'm going to Cannes. *(Pause)* It's nothing, I'm going to Cannes.

(Silence.)

I promised I would. *(Pause)* And besides, I've been drinking a lot, I'm not used . . . He makes me drink.

(Silence.)

At night.

Yes. (*Then, joyfully*) I like it.

(Long silence.)

Yes, intolerable. What?

(Pause) It was necessary, you said so . . .

(After a long pause) No, I didn't understand.

(Silence.)

(Not at once; completely open) I don't know.

(Silence.)

(Distraught at the idea that he's suffering) You used to say it was disgusting . . .

. . . monstrous . . . You wanted this for both of us . . .

(Silence.)

Jean?

You knew it would be difficult, you knew . . .

No. *(Pause)* That's not true. You've known ever since Bordeaux. You just said so.

(Coldly) I shall have gone.

(Not at once) No. *(Pause)* You wouldn't be able to bear it now.

(Silence.

She doesn't answer.)

(Voice faint and dead) Where are you?

Are there a lot of other people?

(Silence.)

I shut myself away here to kill myself, I think.

(He does not reply.)

(Heart-rending smile) And then I went to sleep.

(After a pause) Oh . . . *(A mixture of smiling and childlike plaintiveness)* Perhaps so as not to have to tell lies any more. *(Pause)* You wouldn't have been the only reason . . . *(She stops)*

(Silence.)

Yes?

(She doesn't answer.)

(After a pause) I'm going to meet him now.

(Very long silence.

He doesn't answer.

MICHEL CAYRE *enters noiselessly. Perhaps he has been there for some time, listening. We don't know.* SUZANNA *has sensed his presence and starts to talk conventionally.)*

That was nothing, just now. Just the idea of the summer, I think.

*(*JEAN *doesn't answer. He has realized she's no longer alone.)*

The difference here between the winter and the summer... you can't imagine...

*(*JEAN *is still silent.)*

I went to Les Canoubiers to see the boat... No special reason, just the spur of the moment... *(She stops)* Perhaps I'll go and see Monique in Cannes... or in Juan if she's there.

(Silence.)

I'll let you know anyway. *(Pause)*

(She replaces the phone and turns round. MICHEL *looks at her.)*

BLACKOUT

END OF ACT THREE

39

ACT IV

SUZANNA *is sitting motionless beside the telephone.*
MICHEL CAYRE *is there, quite calm. She turns her
head and sees him, without real surprise. She is still
caught up in her conversation with* JEAN; *over-
whelmed by it. Long pauses in the following
dialogue.*

SUZANNA. *(Very quietly)* Oh. You came.

MICHEL. Yes.

SUZANNA. *(After a pause)* Have you been here long?

MICHEL. Since you saw me. *(Pause)* You were talking
about the summer. *(Pause)* You found it painful to
contemplate. *(Pause)* As if it had been lived through
in advance.

(No answer. Silence.)

SUZANNA. I was just coming to meet you.

MICHEL. *(Still gentle)* How would you have managed
that?

SUZANNA. *(Casting about)* Oh, I'd have rung Riviere
and asked him to come and pick me up. *(Pause,
then quickly)* Or I'd have walked.

MICHEL. You're not late. It's not time yet.

SUZANNA. *(Intake of breath)* I thought...

(Silence.)

MICHEL. No. I was suddenly afraid. So I came...

SUZANNA. *(After a pause)* I wouldn't have stayed
here all night...

*(We should sense the allusion to suicide. No
answer. He goes out on to the terrace. Silence. He
looks at the sea.)*

MICHEL. The sun's still warm.

(She is still stunned and doesn't answer.)

SUZANNA. You've been drinking.

MICHEL. A bit. *(He smiles)* Enough to get us killed on
the road—and us with all those children.

SUZANNA. You drink in the daytime too now...

(She looks at him, from a distance. Silence.)

MICHEL. We can go wherever you like. The car's down the road.

SUZANNA. Strange. I didn't hear you coming.

(Silence. He turns back to the room.)

MICHEL. It was Jean on the phone, wasn't it?

SUZANNA. Yes. *(Long pause)* I'll probably take it. *(Pause)* He told me to do as I liked. *(Pause, then quickly)* I said I'd take it.

(She stands up, leans in the doorway, looks out on the terrace. He looks down on the rocks. Calm. Silence.)

MICHEL. There are some   men going by down below... workmen. *(Pause)* So there *are* a few people.

SUZANNA. *(After a pause)* Just now...two women met each other.. *(Gesture)*..over there. They stopped and talked for quite a while.

(MICHEL *looks at her in surprise, then checks himself. Silence.)*

What were you afraid of?

(No answer. She doesn't press the point. The following dialogue is slow.)

MICHEL. Did you know the two women?

SUZANNA. *(After a pause)* Slightly.

MICHEL. *(After a pause)* Did you hear what they were saying?

SUZANNA. *(After a pause)* Something...

MICHEL. *(After a long pause)* You stood on the terrace and watched them.

SUZANNA. *(Gestures 'Yes')*

MICHEL. For long?

SUZANNA. As long as they were together.

(Long pause.)

Did you see them?

MICHEL. *(Cautiously; he doesn't want to break the thread of the lie)* I think so. *(Pause)* I drove all over the promontory.

(Unusually long pause.)

SUZANNA. Along this road too? *(Pointing)*

(Unusually long pause.)

MICHEL. Yes. *(Pause)* Then I drove on.

SUZANNA. *(After a long pause)* You didn't stay in the room then?

MICHEL. I couldn't. *(Pause, then back to the other theme)* Why did you stand and look at them all that time? *(No answer. He answers for her.)* Because... from a distance, like that, one could imagine they were saying everything? Everything that could be said?

SUZANNA. *(Trying to think)* I think so.

(Silence. He comes back into the room.)

MICHEL. From close to, what were they saying?

SUZANNA. They were lying.

(Silence.)

They spoke about a writer who was killed last week in a car crash. Bernard Fontaine. *(Pause)* Do you know the name?

MICHEL. Vaguely. *(Pause)* Did you know him?

SUZANNA. I met him here. Then I met him again in Paris, like you, two years ago. He asked me to meet him, I remember, in a cafe near the place de l'Alma. I didn't go.

MICHEL. *(After a pause)* Did the women lie about him?

SUZANNA. Not about his death.

(Silence. He looks at the sea.)

MICHEL. There are little inlets. I hadn't noticed.

(Silence.)

SUZANNA. *(After a pause)* Will you come?

MICHEL. *(Jokingly)* Of course. Bag and baggage.

(Silence.)

(With love) Suzanna. *(Pause)* Suzanna.

(She is taken aback. Silence.)

I feel like a swim. Have you seen me swim?

SUZANNA. Once. You're good.

MICHEL. Yes. *(Pause)* One thing I can do. I was champion at the university. *(Self-mocking)* I expect I've told you that before?

(Silence.)

SUZANNA. Yes. *(After a pause. Violent)* Why don't you leave me?

MICHEL. *(After a pause)* I can't yet. I've got so that I couldn't touch another woman.

(Silence.)

Are you afraid?

SUZANNA. What of?

(She doesn't press for an answer. Silence. The allusion is to the end of the affair...Don't be frightened, it won't last, by your own doing... She looks round at the house.)

I think all I really wanted to do was see it. Now, I don't feel it matters any more. This house or another... Perhaps it's always like that when you buy a place, or rent it... at the last moment?

MICHEL. Perhaps. *(Pause)* Do *you* like it?

SUZANNA. *(After a long pause)* I never have an opinion about anything. *(She says this with exasperation, violence. Silence, then she breaks out in a wail)* We'll call at Riviere's and then go. I'll confirm I'm taking it and we'll go back to the hotel. We'll go straight to bed and eat in our room. I'm so tired...

MICHEL. *(After a pause)* No.

(Silence. She realises he's looking at her.)

(Low) What is it?

I'm looking at you.

(Silence. Finally she speaks.)

SUZANNA. *(Slowly, tone of absolute truth)* He asked me if I was in Saint Tropez alone. I said no. He didn't ask me who it was. I'll tell him in a few days. One doesn't know anything but one can always say a name. Michel Cayre. It was the first time we've spoken about it.

(He says nothing. Looks at her. Silence.)

MICHEL.   Did you marry very young?

SUZANNA.   Twenty.

> *(Silence.)*

> *(Starting off again)* He was at Chantilly. *(Pause)*
> He still goes there quite often. *(Pause)* She was out
> for a walk. He was alone in the house.

> *(She looks at him, lowers her eyes, is silent.)*

MICHEL.   It's strange... at first you're not all that
beautiful. And then it's different.

> *(Silence.)*

> I'm trying to see you as a stranger would.

> *(No answer.)*

> I believe what you say. *(Pause)* I believe he
> phoned, too.

> *(Silence.)*

SUZANNA.   *(With difficulty)* I lied about the women
talking.

MICHEL.   No. *(Pause)* On the contrary. *(Pause)* It's a
scene you must have seen often before taking part
in it.

> *(She looks up. Remembers.)*

SUZANNA.   *(After a pause)* In my dreams it was always
by the boat-yard that I met her. *(Pause)* Jean always
came before the dream ended.

MICHEL.   *(Very gently)* Before the murder.

> *(She lowers her eyes. He looks at the house, the
> sea. Silence.)*

> Did he say it was dear?

SUZANNA.   No. *(Pause)* For him it's not all that dear.
For him it's not all that much money.

> *(He looks at her. Slight smile.)*

MICHEL.   *(Gentle)* He would have paid more to lose
you?

SUZANNA.   *(Facing it out; also gently)* Yes. He makes
a lot of money.

> *(Silence. What she said should be touching)*

MICHEL. *(Frankly)* That's the first thing people say about him—that he makes a lot of money.

SUZANNA. Yes.

MICHEL. *(Continuing)* That he makes money very easily.

SUZANNA. *(Gestures 'Yes')* And spends all he makes. A lot of it on women.

MICHEL. *(As if he sees Jean)* To look at him... it's true, he has that grace that money gives.

SUZANNA. *(Looking at* MICHEL, *without aggressiveness)* You can't make money.

MICHEL. No, I can't.

(Silence. Perhaps he's sitting.)

SUZANNA. Wouldn't it interest you?

MICHEL. I've never begun. I don't know.

(Silence.)

SUZANNA. Perhaps he won't come at all this summer.

MICHEL. Would you only have to ask him?

SUZANNA. *(Not answering)* He may come for a couple of days because of the children, but that's all. The rest of the time I don't know where he'll be.

MICHEL. The Balearics.

(Silence.)

SUZANNA. *(She looks astonished, but doesn't go into it)* Oh. *(Pause)* It's possible. *(Pause)* He does what the others do—the people he works with. He goes where they go. The Balearics. Cannes. *(Pause)* Apart from money he hasn't got much imagination. *(Pause)* He's ordinary.

(The blow (about Cannes) was delivered with the utmost gentleness.)

MICHEL. *(Taking it up)* He likes good food. He makes love. He goes for walks in the sun?

SUZANNA. *(With nobility)* I don't know.

(Silence.)

MICHEL. What has he got that I haven't got?

SUZANNA. *(Casts about, then cries out)* But he's got nothing... nothing... that's just it... nothing but money... All he is is rich... apart from that he's... he's poor... he hasn't got anything. Intelligence— he doesn't know anything about it, and doesn't care. He doesn't know anything about you, he doesn't think about you... he doesn't think about anything... He spends all he makes as if... it was going to go on like that for ever... he doesn't think about anything, anything... and I don't care, I prefer...

(Silence. He turns quietly away from her, goes over to the terrace, stops and looks at the sea.)

MICHEL. *(Very gently)* The rocks are in the shadow now. The beach is still in the sun.

(Silence.)

I'd like to love you. *(Pause)* Love you.

SUZANNA. I'm sorry. *(For having cried out)*

MICHEL. Go on, Suzanna, keep on crying out... If only you knew...

SUZANNA. *(Continuing)* The thought of him suffering... He's just a child, you see...

MICHEL. Yes.

SUZANNA. He said I ought to...that it was a shame... and now...

(Silence.)

MICHEL. *(Smiling)* He used to say you were a millstone. That one day he'd give you away.

SUZANNA. *(With a smile)* Yes. *(Pause)* He made bets too. Twice, I think—with pals of his. *(Pause. She looks at him)* Did he do it with you too?

MICHEL. No.

(Silence.

They speak about Jean as if he was a child.)

SUZANNA. He was never without some affair with a woman... never... almost never... When it happened he used to talk about...

(She stops.)

MICHEL. About?

SUZANNA. About separating.

MICHEL. *(After longish pause)* And your affairs were those—Jean's.

SUZANNA. *(After a pause)* Perhaps.

MICHEL. *(Sharply)* You realised it had to happen? What he meant?

SUZANNA. *(After a pause)* No.

(Pause.)

MICHEL. And now?

(No answer.)

(Provocatively) We'll use the room at the top. *(Pause)* We'll have our meals on the terrace. *(Pause)* We'll shut the gate. Nobody will be able to get in.

(SUZANNA *is alarmed, but controls it.)*

SUZANNA. Come when I'm alone.

MICHEL. No.

SUZANNA. *(Diffident)* He never brings anyone.

MICHEL. Couple of Jesuits.

SUZANNA. Yes.

MICHEL. Monique Combes used to go to your place, didn't she?

SUZANNA. But she used to come before. She didn't come so much after.

(He goes out on the terrace.)

MICHEL. The light's fading. It'll soon be dark. *(She doesn't answer)* If I go to Paris now, right away, what will you do?

SUZANNA. Wait three days.

MICHEL. What for?

(No answer. Silence. Then he attacks again.)

(Trying to provoke) We'll put all the furniture in one room. Only keep the beds and the bare walls. Live like that. Alone. For a month. Shut up in the fortress of Les Colonnades.

(She jumps up as if in anguish: is the future

47

ready-made, then?)

I can't do away with the million. But I can do away with the signs—the furniture, the pictures.

SUZANNA. And me?

MICHEL. I might turn you into a novel. That's another way of doing away with your price.

(Silence. She has started up in alarm.)

SUZANNA. Could you?

MICHEL. *(Smiling)* Of course. *(Pause)* I see you as one of those women Michelet talks about *(She listens, still, as before, in alarm)*—in the Middle Ages. *(Pause)* Their husbands were away at the Holy War or the Crusades, and they lived alone for months in a cottage, waiting for them. Months without speaking to anyone. *(Pause)* So they started to talk to trees, to the animals in the forest. People called them witches.

SUZANNA. *(After a pause)* Did they kill them?

MICHEL. Yes. They punished them for holding intelligence with nature. They burned them. *(Long pause)* Their cottages have become your millionaires' houses. *(Pause)* The Crusades have become money. But you haven't got any forest.

(Longish pause.)

SUZANNA. Did *they* believe in God?

MICHEL. *(Smiling)* Yes.

(Pause.

He goes out on to the terrace. Silence.)

You ought to come out. The sun's sinking into the sea.

(She doesn't answer. Doesn't move.)

(After a pause) The harbour's still in the light, but in a minute it will be over.

(As above.)

SUZANNA. You're someone who doesn't want to suffer.

MICHEL. *(After a pause)* That's right. *(He smiles)*
(Silence.)

There! The harbour's in the shadow now.

(Silence.)

No-one wants to suffer, Suzanna.

SUZANNA. Yes, but some people are careful... He just
does everything... *(Pause)* He says things... and
doesn't realise what he's saying. *(Pause)* And then
everything collapses. *(Pause)* And he cries.

(Pause.)

Oh, I know that what's happening to him now has
happened to lots of people...

MICHEL. *(After a pause)* It's feeling the power you
used to have over a woman slip away between your
fingers. Only that.

SUZANNA. *(Absolutely frank)* Yes.

MICHEL. *(More blows)* It's soon over. A month and it's
finished. Consoled.

SUZANNA. Yes.

(Silence.)

(Continued delirium) I believe Monique Combes is
wrong if she hopes he'll go with her... *I* think he'll
go with the one with the house at Chantilly. *(Long
pause)* I've seen her photograph in the papers—
she's younger and prettier than Monique... at least,
I think so.

(Silence, all MICHEL's efforts have been vain.)

MICHEL. *(Softly)* You make me want to kill you. And
at the same time I see how you can enter right into
someone... and stay there.

(Silence, then it resumes.)

SUZANNA. He couldn't tell *me* about the Balearics, of
course... *(Pause)* So you've seen him since the
summer... you didn't say anything?

MICHEL. *(After a pause)* Everyone knows, Suzanna.

SUZANNA. What?

MICHEL. That your lover's Michel Cayre. Jean knows
too. Everyone pretended not to for your sake.

(Silence.)

SUZANNA. *(After a pause)* What?

49

MICHEL. *(Not answering)* Come, Suzanna, come over here with me.

SUZANNA. *(Signs 'No')*

MICHEL. You don't want to. *(Pause)* Oh well. *(Long pause)* He rang me up a couple of months ago. Said he had something to say to me. We met when he'd finished at the office. *(Pause)* He said what he wanted to tell me was not to hurt you. That he wouldn't forgive me if I did. *(Pause)* It was after that that we talked about the holidays and he told me he was going to the Balearics this summer.

(SUZANNA *is silent while she reconstructs her universe. Then smiles gently.)*

SUZANNA. Always afraid someone's going to hurt me... it's ridiculous...

(Silence. The reconstruction has been done.)

Jean's like that, you see. He thinks he's listening. But he's not listening at all. *(Pause)* He was told... but he didn't believe it... or rather... yes, that's it... he thinks he knows, but he doesn't know at all.

(Silence.)

(Smiling) I expect he asked you not to say anything to me?

MICHEL. Yes. *(Pause)* I gave him my word of honour.

SUZANNA. *(After a pause)* Why did you tell me? *(She doesn't wait for an answer)* But why not. He didn't know anything until today.

MICHEL. You're right. Nothing. Neither did you. Neither did I.

(Silence.)

SUZANNA. *(Trying to think)* What was it you didn't know?

MICHEL. What you'd be like faced with Jean's pain.

(Silence. It's as if she didn't any longer quite understand what's said to her.)

SUZANNA. *(Absolutely natural)* Are the Balearics beautiful?

(We see him, in the distance, bury his head in his hands and cry out. Complete sincerity.)

MICHEL. I love you, Suzanna. I love you and I'm glad
of it. It's killing me and I don't care. I love you...

(Silence, she is alarmed. Still. He answers.)

Yes, it's beautiful there. The sea is warm. *(Pause)*
It's very hot, too hot for children.

SUZANNA. So I'd heard...

*(Silence. He is in the same strange condition. He
doesn't look at her any more. He wants to hear her
speak of love.)*

MICHEL. Talk to me about him. Talk to me.

(Surprised and on her guard, she is silent.)

(Trying to encourage her) He's stayed very young—
he doesn't know how to suffer?

SUZANNA. No.

MICHEL. I've only seen him happy. I suppose he
suffers in the same way as he's happy? All out.

SUZANNA. *(Still mistrustful)* Yes, that's right. *(Pause)*
He goes to bed. He won't eat. Wants to die. *(Pause)*
He'll be like that this evening.

MICHEL. The pain was there, hanging over him,
waiting for your voice. The voice of the unknown
Suzanna Andler. He'd forgotten she existed.
(Pause) Can you see him?

SUZANNA. Yes. *(Pause)* I've seen him suffer over
other women. Often.

MICHEL. Did he want to come down here right away,
tonight?

SUZANNA. Yes. He wanted to fly. *(Pause)* I said no.
(Pause) What's the point of coming? What
difference would it make?

MICHEL. None.

(Silence.)

I can see him too, Jean Andler, the moneymaker.
I can see him better than myself... a lost soul, a
puppet. I can see him through you.

SUZANNA. *(After a pause)* Would you kill him if you
could? *(He doesn't answer)* If you had the power,
would you kill him? *(In the French she uses the
formal 'Vous' instead of the familiar 'Tu' in the
last sentence.)*

MICHEL. *(Smiling)* What does he think?

SUZANNA. *(After a pause)* Nothing. He doesn't think about it.

MICHEL. No, not kill him. Put him in a factory. Take his money and his children away from him and chuck him in among all the Portuguese. He'd be swallowed up and forgotten.

SUZANNA. *(After a pause)* No. It would start all over again. *(Longish pause)* He'd work, take an interest, work harder and harder, and it would start all over again. No, that wouldn't be any good. *(Long pause)* No, if you want to get rid of him the only way is to kill him. Or shut him up in prison where he can't do anything or see anybody. Nothing. Nobody.

(Silence. It's in fact as if she had just been speaking of her love. She weeps.)

Perhaps that might do it.

(You can tell from her voice that she's crying.)

MICHEL. *(Low)* Suzanna. Suzanna, come.

(She doesn't answer. Silence. Then the sound of a siren. She starts up.)

SUZANNA. What's that?

MICHEL. The siren at the powder-mill. It's six o'clock.

(The pain bursts out.)

SUZANNA. And I've been here since this morning. What for? What for?

(He doesn't answer.)

(Agitated) Riviere was supposed to phone... I don't understand...I suppose he couldn't contact the owners, that's why he's late... Well, we can call at his place... we're not just going to hang around waiting...

(No answer.)

Let's go.

MICHEL. No need. *(Pause)* The house has already been taken.

(She is rooted to the spot. Then starts to go towards the terrace.)

Jean telephoned Riviere this morning after he saw

52

you. The cheque's already in the post. *(Pause)* I met Monique Combes at lunch-time. She told me. *(Pause)* It's all fixed.

(SUZANNA *has approached close behind* MICHEL. *He turns and sees her frozen in the act of pushing him. He looks intensely astonished.)*

(Low) You were there...

(There is nothing to be read in her eyes. She is the first to move. She comes back into the room. He follows. Silence. She looks round at the house.)

SUZANNA. *(A long-drawn-out wail like one uttered in sleep)* It's as if I'd been living here for months... I'd thought of it as quite different... I went to Clair-Bois for too long. *(She turns to him, explaining what she has explained before)* The house we used to go to... It had got to be a home. *(Long pause)* I'd rather have a garden than those awful rocks... *(She looks at the sea)* The dusk is depressing by the Mediterranean... and you can see... you can see too much of it. *(Pause)* Perhaps it's the time of day that makes the place look so depressing?

MICHEL. It's a terrible time everywhere.

(She turns and looks around the house.)

SUZANNA. It belongs to some people in Nice. The Jacquemonts. They've more or less broken up, according to Riviere. They had this place built and then... They never come here.

(Silence.)

Something is supposed to have happened here... A few years ago... three years perhaps... haven't you heard about it?

(No answer.)

The wife tried to kill herself...*(Pause)*... or someone tried to kill her...I don't remember...Jean would know...I don't remember...

MICHEL. *(Gentle)* Try.

SUZANNA. *(Trying to get out of it)* Unless people were just making it up...

(Silence. They look at each other.)

(Low) Strange... I hardly recognise you.

(Silence.)

Just now... *(She stops)*

MICHEL.   *(Softly, as if his thoughts too were elsewhere)*
What did you see?

SUZANNA.   *(Describing what she saw)* You'd fallen
face down, I was looking at you. I think you were
dead.

MICHEL.   No. *(Pause)* I can't die.

(She looks at him in astonishment.)

(Gently) You meant everyone had stopped speaking.
(Pause) The house was silent again.

SUZANNA.   *(As if absent-mindedly)* Strange. Just
because of a word. The word "cheque". The
cheque signed and posted...

MICHEL.   *(Impacably)* The irrevocable. *(Pause)* The
lover with a name. The house with a name. The
summer fixed.

SUZANNA.   *(Still with the same strange absent-
mindedness)* Yes... as if it couldn't be undone...

MICHEL.   *(After a pause)* Yes.

(After a pause) Yes.

(Silence. Calm.)

SUZANNA.   I could still destroy it all. I could go to
Riviere and tell him I've changed my mind... that
Jean didn't realise, but that...? Les Colonnades...
no... couldn't I?

MICHEL.   *(After a pause)* I don't think there'd be any
difficulty. *(Pause)* All you have to do is decide
now.

SUZANNA.   *(Trying to do so)* Unless I just leave it...
Either we'll spend the summer here... *(Pause)* Or
else... if... then it'll just stay empty... What do you
think?

(He doesn't answer. It's all one to him.

Silence. She looks outside.)

(An age-old instinct) We'd better shut the
windows.

MICHEL.   Why?

SUZANNA. It'll soon be dark.

MICHEL. Leave them open.

SUZANNA: What about burglars? ... tramps get into the grounds at night.

(He doesn't answer.)

The electricity's cut off—we shall soon be in the dark.

MICHEL. Let's go.

SUZANNA. Where? Cannes?

MICHEL. If you like. Or if you like we can stay here. *(Pause)* It's of no importance. *(Pause)* We'll wait three days. Then we'll go back.

SUZANNA. Just to give him time to get used to it...

MICHEL. *(Stopping her)* Yes.

(At last she looks at him, for himself.)

SUZANNA. What will your novel be about?

MICHEL. Love.

SUZANNA. *(Intake of breath)* Oh...

MICHEL. The story of an impossible love. An agony. *(Pause)* Any other love would be more tempting. It would be blind. It would have the innocence of monsters, their crushing weight. It would advance for ever, without knowledge, without thought, in a prehistory endless and fathomless. And it would get greater and greater.

(She listens. He smiles, piercingly.)

One would watch it living, advancing. *(Pause)* Realise there was no point in trying to stop it. *(Pause)* And perhaps in that way one might be able to enter into it.

(Silence. She ponders.)

SUZANNA. *(Trying to understand; completely frank)* I don't quite understand. *(Pause)* I don't read enough... I really don't read at all.

(He doesn't answer.)

But as you won't be writing it for me...

(She tries again to understand.)

Who would watch?

(He can't answer.)

Perhaps you don't know yet?

(No answer. She doesn't press it. She looks outside. Long silence.)

Was it fine here today?

MICHEL.   I think so.

SUZANNA.   In Paris it was awful. Storms. Wind. *(Pause)* Of course it'll soon be March.

(He doesn't answer. She starts going.)

Christine's going to England this year. I shall only have the two younger ones. Marc's very easy to manage... But Irene...

(They are gone. We hear their voices but the stage is empty.)

She's a very difficult child to understand... She tells lies... Oh, only little ones... but it's hard to see why... She has everything she wants, and yet she tells lies... Jean says we just ought to leave her alone...

CURTAIN

La Musica

LA MUSICA was first produced by the London Traverse Company at the Jeanetta Cochrane Theatre with the following cast:

ANNE-MARIE ROCHE (SHE)	Joanna Dunham
MICHEL NOLLET (HE)	Sandor Eles

The entrance hall of a hotel. Street noises. To the left, two notices: 'Reception'; 'Dining Room'. A clear space inside the entrance, but to the right, reaching past the centre of the stage, the hall is arranged as a conventional hotel lounge, with settee and armchairs, desk, and a television set placed so that people watching it can be seen while the screen remains invisible.

We hear certain members of the hotel staff but never see them: no point in cluttering up the stage with the antique presence of waiters and manageresses.

The two main characters are quite ordinary in appearance; there is nothing about them to attract special attention.

The staging should be cinematic, with the faces strongly lit for the equivalent of close-ups and occasionally plunged in darkness. The rest of the stage should grow gradually darker as the dialogue progresses.

MICHEL NOLLET *enters left and crosses to the reception desk, which is out of sight. We hear the following conversation off.*

HE.   Excuse me. Are you sure the nine-sixteen is still the only train for Paris?

OLD LADY.   I'm afraid so, Monsieur Nollet. Next year they're going to start an air service three times a week, but in the meanwhile...Here's your key.

HE.   I'm not going up, thanks. Could you get me a call to Paris? The number is Littré 89-26.

O.L.   Littré 89-26. Certainly, Monsieur Nollet. Shall I put it through to you in the lounge?

HE.   *(Hesitating)* ...Yes, if you will, please.

(HE *comes back into the lounge and stands by the desk, waiting.)*

O.L.   This is the Hotel de France, Evreux. Could I have Paris, Littré 89-26, please, and could you tell me how long it will take? *(Pause)* How long? *(Calling to* MICHEL NOLLET) It'll be through in five minutes, Monsieur Nollet.

(Longish pause. Then ANNE-MARIE ROCHE *enters. She too crosses to reception.* HE *reacts when he sees her, but does his best not to show it. She doesn't see him.)*

O.L.   There's a telegram for you, Madame...*(Embarrassed)* Madame Nollet.

SHE.   *(Quite calmly)* Ah yes? I was expecting it.

(HE, *as well as the audience, is listening to the conversation.)*

O.L.   Here's your key, Madame.

SHE.   Thank you, I'm not going up. I just dropped in for the telegram...I thought I'd go for a walk.

O.L.   You'll be surprised how much the place has changed. You can hardly recognize it around the station.

SHE.   What about out at...out at La Boissière?

O.L.   *(Embarrassed)* La B--? Oh, I believe that's still much the same... But of course I don't go out much and I hardly ever get as far as that...

SHE.   Well, I shan't be long.

O.L.   Very well, madame.

(Pause. ANNE-MARIE *comes back into the lounge, putting the telegram into her bag. She sees* MICHEL NOLLET *and stops. He looks at her and bows slightly. She just perceptibly nods in acknowledgement.)*

HE.   I just wanted to say...if there was anything you wanted me to do...*(Strained smile)*...like the furniture that's in store...I could arrange for it to be sent if you like, to save you the trouble.

SHE.   Furniture? *(Then* SHE *remembers)* Oh yes. No, thank you. *(Pause)* I don't know yet what I shall be doing...whether I want to keep it or not... But thank you. *(Pause)* Goodnight.

HE.   Goodnight.

(SHE *goes out. Left alone,* HE *lights a cigarette, still standing.* HE *is agitated, but has himself almost completely under control. The telephone rings.)*

O.L.   Hallo? Is that Littré 89-26? Your call, Monsieur Nollet.

(We hear the voice at the other end of the line, muted but quite clearly audible.)

WOMAN'S VOICE.   Is that you, Michel?

HE.   Yes...How are you?

W.V.   I'm all right. *(Pause)* Is it all over?

HE.   Yes.

W.V.   When?

HE.   This afternoon.

W.V.   I...I hope it wasn't too...painful.

HE.   Well...No, it was all right.

(Silence. HE can't make conversation.)

W.V.   Did...did you see her?

HE.   Of course.

W.V.   ...And?

HE.   Nothing. *(Pause)* What do you want me to say? *(Slightly mocking)* That's life, as they say... Getting a divorce...It's bound to be...
(Pause)

W.V.   What?

HE.   *(Ironical)* Well, let's say it's never easy.

W.V.   Has...has she changed?

HE.   *(It's a question he hasn't asked himself)* Yes...I suppose so. Yes.
(Pause)

W.V.   Michel. Do you love me?

HE.   *(Without hesitation, sincerely, but automatically)* Yes. I do. *(Pause)* Tomorrow then at three-seventeen at the Gare Saint-Lazare?

W.V.   Yes, I'll wait at the main exit, that's the safest. *(Pause)* We could go to the cinema in the evening if you like...

HE.   If you like.
(Pause)

61

W.V. *(With a sort of uneasiness, impatience)* Will you tell me about it one day?

(Pause)

HE. I don't think so...but...who knows? One day, perhaps.

W.V. But why?

(HE *doesn't answer)*

W.V. Forgive me.

HE. It's nothing...*(To change the subject)* What are you doing this evening, sweetheart?

W.V. Nothing. I've been in bed all day. *(Pause)* Where is she staying?

HE. (HE *hesitates, restrains himself)* I don't know.

W.V. Have you had dinner?

HE. No. I thought I'd ring you before I went. This is the back of beyond. Everyone's in bed by nine.

W.V. Will you take me there one day?

HE. *(A little laugh)* Yes, why not? *(Pause)* Well, see you tomorrow, sweetheart. Goodnight.

W.V. Good night, Michel.

*(*HE *goes out. The entrance hall remains empty. A light is turned out. A clock is heard theatrically striking ten.*

ANNE-MARIE ROCHE *comes in, smoking a cigarette. She wanders round the lounge, sees the television set, switches on and sits down to watch. We hear the end of the news.*

HE *comes in.* SHE *doesn't hear. He stands and looks at her; remembering something; with intense emotion. He looks at her: she is free again. He hesitates and finally goes and sits down behind her. She senses somebody there and turns round. The following dialogue goes very slowly.)*

SHE. Oh!...it's you.

HE. *(Getting up)* Why shouldn't we talk to each other?

SHE. Why should we?

HE. No particular reason...because we haven't got anything else to do.

62

(SHE *gives a grimace of distaste, bitterness, sadness.)*

SHE.   Nothing could be more over and done with than... than that.

HE.   *(Hesitates, then)* We could be dead...Or were you including death?

(HE *smiles,* SHE *doesn't.)*

SHE.   I don't know...But perhaps, yes...perhaps including death.

(HE *doesn't pursue it.* SHE *didn't want to speak in the first place, but goes on now to try to get rid of this constraint.)*

SHE.   Thanks for offering about the furniture. I've thought about it...I don't want it...it'll just be in the way...But if you'd like it...*(Pause)* We don't have to stick to the *(slight laugh)* legal division.

HE.   *(Slight laugh)* No, no thanks...*(Thinking about something else)* No, I don't want anything.

(Pause)

SHE.   What shall we do with it then?

HE.   *(Still thinking of something else)* I don't know. Nothing. Just leave it there...

SHE.   *(Smiling)* Right.

(Silence.)

HE.   Would you like a drink?

(SHE *gestures 'Why not?'* HE *walks over towards reception and looks, without going off. Comes back.)*

HE.   *(Smiling)* Sorry, I think they've all gone to bed.

SHE.   *(Smiling)* It doesn't matter.

(SHE *gets up. They don't quite know where to go from here. The banality of the following dialogue is exaggerated.*[1]*)*

HE.   *(Trying to keep it light)* The place is completely changed—have you seen?

SHE.   It hasn't changed much out at La Boissière.

HE.   No...it's more towards the north, the development out towards where they're building the new

(1)   This passage can be extended or cut, or modified.

aerodrome. You heard about that?

SHE.   Yes, it'll be a great improvement—change everything.

HE.   Did you go out there...to La Boissière?

SHE.   *(Looking at him in surprise)* Yes, of course. I've
never been back here since...(SHE *smiles)* You've
just come back from there, haven't you?

HE.   *(Surprised and confused)* How did you know?

SHE.   I thought I saw you at the top of the hill when I
got there...But I wasn't sure...

HE.   *(Looking away)* Yes, I went past the house.
(Embarrassed pause) I didn't think the couple that
bought it from us were so young as that, did you?

SHE.   No...it must have changed hands again since...I
didn't recognise the two people who were having
dinner there tonight.

HE.   *(Smiling)* Yes...it was strange...the dining room was
arranged just as...just as it used to be. Even the
television...

SHE.   *(Continuing)* And they weren't saying anything
to each other...not a word...yes, strange...

(Slight laugh. Silence.)

HE.   They've finished the block of flats I started. Do
you remember? Out beyond the race-course?

SHE.   I don't think I...Oh yes, I remember! Have they
made a good job of it?

HE.   Yes...it looks as though they kept to the plans.

(What can they say? HE makes another effort.)

HE.   I suppose I ought to have come back now and
again to make sure they were getting on all right...
But I didn't...Anyway, it's not too bad.

SHE.   Is your work still going well?

HE.   Not too badly, thanks. I've had a couple of very
good commissions lately.

SHE.   Are you still as mad about it as ever?

*(SHE smiles. She must have been jealous of his
work in the past.)*

HE.   *(Smiling too)* Yes, as mad as ever.

SHE.   Good.

HE.   Thanks. *(Pause)* I suppose you're catching the
      nine-sixteen in the morning?

SHE.   *(Hesitating)* No. Someone's fetching me.

      (Silence.)

HE.   It's funny...I don't even know where you live...
      Someone asked me how you were the other day
      and I couldn't tell him.

SHE.   Oh, I'm not really living anywhere for the moment...
      all over the place...mostly in the north...

HE.   The north!

SHE.   Yes...that's how it turned out...I quite like it.

HE.   *(With a smile that's already warm)* You still hate
      the south as much as ever?

SHE.   Yes, as much as ever.

      *(Silence. They move to different places and the
      conversation changes direction.)*

HE.   I haven't heard anything about you for two years.

SHE.   Valerie gives me news about you every so often...

HE.   *(Starting slightly)* Do you still see her?

SHE.   Yes...I...I think quite differently about her now.
      You...without being exactly prejudiced, it's not
      that, you can get into the habit of adopting
      someone else's views...you...without realising it
      you're under their influence...*(Pause)* I see the
      Tourniers sometimes too. *(Pause)* That's all, I
      think.

      *(These allusions, which are never repeated or
      explained, are to their common past.)*

HE.   *(Risking it)* I didn't think you'd come alone. I
      thought you'd have someone with you.

SHE.   *(With a shrug)* No...*(Pause)* You came alone too...

HE.   Yes...I didn't think there was any point...

SHE.   No...

      (SHE *indicates that she didn't think there was any
      point either. They both smile very faintly. They look
      at each other properly for the first time. Enormous
      feeling of constraint; but curiosity is even stronger.)*

HE.　...Do you really mean, including death?

(The dialogue goes very slowly here, SHE *doesn't answer.)*

You said that nothing was more over and done with than...than that. Even death.

SHE.　I said I didn't know.

HE.　*(Laughing)* You know when you came back from Paris...I was waiting for you on the platform...

(SHE *looks at him.* HE *looks down, stops laughing, doesn't go on. She gets up from her chair and walks about the room. He is not surprised that she cannot keep still. While she is still standing he presses it even further.)*

HE.　*(Sudden but polite)* Are you going to get married again?

SHE.　*(Equally abrupt)* What happened on the platform?

(Silence. HE *hesitates, says nothing.* SHE *doesn't press it. Something resembling the old violence has just passed between them.)*

SHE.　I'm getting married again in August.

HE.　Three months. . .

SHE.　Yes, the legal interval. . .it's stupid, but what can you do?

HE.　Yes.

SHE.　*(Letting him have it but still not in an unseemly way)* We shall be going away afterwards. Going to live in America. *(Pause)* I want...peace and quiet... A bit late, I know, even for that...I've got to be quick, to make up for lost time...

(Polite smile)

HE.　So you think, now, that time doesn't always have to be lost?

SHE.　Just a manner of speaking...I've never thought about it...Really, never.

(SHE *restrains a laugh.)* And what are you going to do?

HE.　Much the same as you, except that I have to stay in France because of my work.

SHE.　Will you get married again?

HE. I don't know yet.

(HE *takes her in completely, from head to foot.*
SHE *doesn't see.*)

HE. *(Almost involuntarily)* You haven't changed.

(SHE *turns round quite suddenly, we see her face.*)

SHE. I've aged, I know...

HE. I didn't mean...

(They are stirred.)

HE. Yes, you have changed a bit in the face.

SHE. How?

HE. I think it's the eyes chiefly...You used to have a
very...gentle way of looking at people...and then as
soon as they looked at you they could guess, more
or less, what you were going to say.

SHE. *(Stiffly)* That must have been very boring.

(SHE *pretends to laugh.*)

HE. At the end, yes. During the last few months, very
boring indeed.

(SHE *goes over and switches on the television.*
Nothing happens, the programme has closed down.
She looks at her watch.)

SHE. Eleven o'clock already.

(Perhaps HE hasn't heard.)

HE. It's amazing, you and I standing here talking like
this... (HE *indicates himself and her with his hand*)
Do you remember those last months?

(At last, they both burst out laughing.)

SHE. Hell.

HE. Yes. Hell.

(SHE *shuts her eyes and tries with a wave of the*
hand to efface the image of what she sees. They
gradually stop laughing.)

SHE. I shouldn't think it could be as bad as that more
than once in a lifetime, should you?

HE. What?

SHE. That hell.

HE. I shouldn't think so. *(Pause)* Or else...

(We feel something stir between them again, but this time neither tries to get free of it.)

HE. Or else experience, that beastly experience we hear so much about, is absolutely useless...

SHE. No...you're wrong, I think...it's not that...If it happens again...I've thought about it since...if it happens again it must be because one hasn't discovered any other way of...

(SHE *tries to find the words.)*

HE. *(Finding them)*...of escaping from...fatigue, perhaps?

SHE. *(Eyes lowered)* Yes, I think that's it. *(Pause)* Don't you?

HE. Perhaps.

(Silence. Memories crowd upon them more and more vividly.)

SHE. *(Trying to remember)* How long was it we stayed here in the hotel before we moved into the house? I can't remember how long it was before it was ready—three months? Six?

HE. *(Trying to remember)* About three, I think...

(It was here in the Hôtel de France that the rarest part of their life together took place. They fall quite silent.)

SHE. Isn't it strange we should find it so hard to remember?

HE. Some...moments come back more clearly than others...But I think what lies behind them counts just as much...you can't always tell.

SHE. *(Quite directly, but as if she were speaking about memory in general and not theirs in particular)* And there are some moments that are absolutely clear.

HE. *(The same)* Hell, for example?

SHE. Perhaps...

HE. Good times after bad?...Reconciliations...Isn't that what you mean?

SHE. Yes.

(SHE *seems to be trying to disperse the growing
feeling between them by talking.*)

If the story of every couple were governed by its
own particular laws...and I believe it is...if every...
couple has its own fundamental way of...and I
believe it has...then we ought never have moved
into the house...never have...settled down...we
ought to have stayed on here in the hotel.

HE. *(Continuing her thought)* And lived just like that...
going from one hotel to another...like people in
hiding?...like...

SHE. Perhaps...

(*Silence. Muffled explosion: what* HE *was going to
say was 'like lovers'.*)

Don't you think...?

HE. Yes...but then there was no reason why we should
behave differently from everyone else. We were
young, everyone approved of our getting married...
Everyone was happy, your family, my family,
everyone...We had everything we needed (HE
laughs), house, furniture...your fur coat...

SHE. We behaved just like everyone else. Yes.

HE. But we *were* just like everyone else, so there was
no reason why we shouldn't have done...what's usual...
the same as them.

SHE. And so we've finished up at the same point.

HE. Is that a question?

SHE. Perhaps...

(*Pause*)

HE. Yes, I think we have finished up at the same point
as the others. Sometimes there's a divorce,
sometimes not...but perhaps...perhaps the difference
is negligible.

SHE. If it hadn't been now it would have been later...

(HE *doesn't answer.*)

Don't you think?

HE. What?

SHE. The...end...Don't you think?

HE.   How can you say when...you haven't tried...

SHE.   Yes, you can have an idea. Besides, what does it matter whether something lasts a long time or a short time...if it's got to end anyway...That's what one has to tell oneself...

HE.   In that case *(smiling),* everything is working out according to the rules.

SHE.   Yes, of course. That too...

(They are silent.)

(Very low) How stupid...

HE.   What?

SHE.   *(Correcting, herself)* No. It's true—it's... automatic...

HE.   ...You're starting all over again...I'm starting all over again...

(SHE *reacts involuntarily.)*

SHE.   Yes, but...

HE.   *(Continuing her sentence)...* this time we know that the end is inevitable?

(SHE *doesn't answer.)*

No?

SHE.   Yes...and no. We know that a certain kind of end is inevitable.

HE.   *(With difficulty)* A certain kind?

SHE.   Yes. The only kind...But we also know there's no need to shout it from the rooftops...we know you can dispense with *(slight laugh)* the third act.

HE.   We were extremely young.

SHE.   And now we don't want all that trouble, all that worry, we...

HE.   *(Interrupting)* We've got other things to do?

SHE.   I suppose so.

HE.   What?

SHE.   *(Laughing)* Nothing. But I expect we've got a different way of doing it. *(Pause)* We used not to shrink from anything...at the drop of a hat there'd be sleepless nights, scenes, tragedies...

(They laugh.)

HE. Violence.

(SHE *hesitates and then confesses.)*

SHE. And even worse...

(The allusion is to an attempt at suicide.

HE *is dumbfounded. He gets up and comes over to her. The second act of* 'La Musica': *she almost died, and he discovers it.)*

HE. What?

SHE. Yes *(She laughs)*, oh, yes.

HE. When?

SHE. *(Looking at him)* When you asked for a divorce. But it wasn't really serious...After all, here I still am...it must have been just a vulgar attempt at blackmail.

(Clock theatrically strikes midnight. HE is rooted to the spot by what he has just heard.)

HE. *(Just a murmur)* I had no idea...

SHE. *(Low)* How could you have? It was inconsistent, I know, but I asked them not to say anything to you.

HE. *(Involuntarily)* But...it's terrible!

SHE. *(Smiling)* No, it's nothing...the idiotic sort of thing everyone does. *(Pause. HE says nothing)* I shouldn't have told you...

HE. No...no...I'm sorry.

(SHE *tries to change the subject, and at the same time to find out about him.)*

SHE. Valèrie's spoken to me about...her. She's...very young, isn't she?

HE. Yes.

SHE. *(Absently)* You don't know him...you've never met.

HE. And...

SHE. *(Understanding he means does she love the other man)* Yes. Everything is all right. Everything is as it should be...

71

(They fall silent again. It is growing late. The memories crowd upon them.)

SHE.   *(Slowly, painfully)* We must go up. They're waiting to turn out the lights.

(SHE *points towards reception.)*

HE.   *(Roughly)* Let them wait.

(Long silence.)

SHE.   No point in talking like that. We must go up.

HE.   *(Using her name for the first time)* Anne-Marie... it's the last time in our lives.

(SHE *doesn't answer, but remains seated. They are silent a full minute. Then with a sharp but not unprepared transition, she begins to speak.)*

SHE.   *(There is an element of challenge in her voice)* He was another man, not you. That was the main thing—he was another. On one side there was just you, and on the other there were all the men that I should never know. *(Pause)* I think you must understand me quite clearly. *(Pause)* Don't you?

HE.   Yes.

SHE.   I was sure you would. *(Pause)* I think that at the moment...we were quits.

HE.   *(Crisply)* Yes, we were that. *(Pause)* It's funny to to hear the truth two years afterwards.

SHE.   Interesting.

HE.   I never knew...what happened that time you went to Paris. What you told me...then...I don't suppose that was the truth.

SHE.   You wouldn't have been able to bear the truth. Now at this distance, you think you could have. But you couldn't.

HE.   I couldn't bear anything.

(Attempt at a laugh.)

SHE.   Hardly anything. *(Pause)* Nothing.

(Pause)

HE.   *(With difficulty)* How did...did it happen?

SHE.   Oh, do we have to talk about it?

HE.   No reason why we shouldn't indulge in the truth now.

SHE. *(After an effort to remember)* I met him standing up on a bus. *(Pause. She is almost reciting)* Afterwards he waited outside my hotel. I saw him there once, twice...the third time I was frightened, it was late, he was outside the hotel still, it was almost one o'clock in the morning and... there you are.

HE. *(Roughly)* Where had you been?

SHE. A night-club in Saint-Germain-des-Prés. *(Pause)* You didn't know about that either, did you?

HE. No.

SHE. I used to go dancing sometimes...You didn't dance...I missed it, I think I must have missed it a good deal.

HE. It would have been all the same if I had danced.

SHE. Probably. *(A silence)* You know, it's quite terrible the first time you're unfaithful...awful. *(She laughs)* It's true...the first time...even if it's only...quite casual...it's awful. It's quite wrong to say it's unimportant.

(HE *is silent, smiling vaguely.)*

(Going on) I don't think that for a man being unfaithful is ever so...serious...

HE. Was it because of him you put off coming back?

SHE. Yes.

HE. *(Painfully)* Did you want it to happen or did it happen in spite of you?

SHE. I wanted it. I was desperate. I did it to try to recapture the first moments...the first time. That was all. Like you I did it to recapture those moments...that can never be replaced. *(Pause)* But you know, the taste for that sort of adventure... you get it from someone else...

HE. I'm glad you wanted it to happen...I don't care about the rest. *(Slowly, with difficulty)* And did you recapture the first moments?

SHE. One always does...even...at the worst...even only for an hour...you know that as well as I do...That was why I didn't want to come back. No other reason.

(Silence. HE *is trying to look back beyond what*

happened in Paris.)

HE.   One afternoon, a few months before you went to
         Paris, I...I saw you...you didn't see me...You were
         going along the street there (HE *points outside)*
         and I followed you...It was in the afternoon. I'd
         left the office to go and look at one of the building
         sites, and I saw you going into a cinema...

SHE.   *(Laughing)* Oh, yes!

HE.   *(Laughing too)* I followed you in. They were
         showing a western that we'd already seen together...
         You were alone...near the front...no-one came and
         sat with you...That evening you didn't say anything
         about it...and I didn't ask any questions...It was
         spring, three years ago...you were sad sometimes
         already...The next day, after lunch, I asked if you
         were going out. You said no, but you did. I
         followed you again. You went to the races...still
         alone. I'd never dreamed...*(Pause)* I started to
         suffer.

         (A silence. SHE remembers.)

SHE.   Yes, I used to do things like that.

HE.   *(With a smile)* And do you still?

SHE.   *(Laughing)* Yes.

HE.   I had you followed every day for a week.

SHE.   And you didn't find anybody.

HE.   No. Not that that made any difference.

         (Pause.)

         (Resuming) It was terrible. I was jealous of you
         yourself...of that secret part of you...One day I
         followed you by car. You looked marvellous,
         there alone in your car. You were driving very
         fast...You drove out about twenty kilometers and
         pulled up by a wood. You went into the wood and
         I lost sight of you. I hesitated and almost came
         after you, and then...I just drove away. That's one
         of the absolutely clear memories that we were
         talking about just now.

SHE.   But it's nothing, nothing at all, it's just my way
         of passing the time. *(Pause)* I'd forgotten that
         drive. *(Pause)* But you ought to have come and
         found me...

HE. I was afraid of being in the way...I thought you wanted to be on your own.

SHE. Yes, I did, sometimes.

HE. Don't defend yourself.

SHE. I'm not.

HE. There's no need...I was still a bit intrigued by it, that's all.

SHE. *(Almost as she might have said it 'before')* You are funny. Why shouldn't one do things like that?

HE. No reason at all. But why say nothing about them?

SHE. There's no point.

HE. That's not true.

SHE. *(Bluntly, in the present)* I've never seen the use of talking about things like that, and yet strangely enough...

HE. *(Insisting)* You could say, in the evening: I went to the cinema this afternoon.

(SHE *thinks for a moment.*)

SHE. No. You see, you don't do that sort of thing at... at the beginning...so when you do start to do it it's better not to talk about it...It would be misunderstood, wouldn't it...

HE. Misunderstood?

SHE. Oh, some people spend the afternoon weeping when love starts to languish...I go to the races.

(The light sinks lower. The clock theatrically strikes two. The room is almost in darkness. They don't move.)

SHE. *(Very low)* Two o'clock. What will people think?

(HE *doesn't answer.*

The return of desire.

HE *gets up as if he has made up his mind to leave it at that, and goes slowly over towards reception.* SHE *remains seated.)*

HE. *(Turning round)* What number is your key?

SHE. Twenty-eight.

(SHE *gets up too. He comes back and they stand*

75

*facing each other. He holds out her key. They do
not move, she doesn't take it. He speaks very
softly, assuming an unreal tone.)*

HE. *(Very gentle)* This is very silly. You'll be exhausted
tomorrow. *(Pause)* What time are you being called
for?

SHE. I don't know exactly—some time before nine.

HE. Goodbye.

SHE. Goodbye.

(SHE *takes the key and they start to go off in
opposite directions. But after a few steps they
both stand still.*

HE *comes back; she is leaning against a chair,
watching him. They are face to face.)*

SHE. *(Harshly)* What happened on the platform?

HE. I wanted to kill you. I'd bought a gun and I was
going to kill you as you got off the train.

SHE. In such cases the murderer is usually acquitted.
Did you know that?

HE. I knew.

*(Silence. Anger. Despair. They stand stiff and
motionless.)*

SHE. Why didn't you do it?

HE. I don't remember.

SHE. That's not true.

HE. It is. I've forgotten.

SHE. *(Insistent)* Try to remember. You disappeared
from the house that night without saying anything.

HE. Just a minute...Ah yes, I drove to Cabourg. When I
got there I threw the revolver in the sea. I thought
that was what one did with a revolver...(HE
laughs) I'd read it somewhere.

SHE. *(Grim)* Had you read about violence too?

HE. About that too.

SHE. *(Confesses)* And I'd read about committing
adultery in Paris.

(Silence.)

76

SHE. *(Exaggerated tone of aggressiveness)* Well, what are we going to do about the furniture?

HE. Nothing.

SHE. That's absurd.

HE. Yes...I don't know...

(It's clear that they are thinking about something else.)

HE. Did you want it to happen, or did it happen by chance?

SHE. *(Taken aback at first)* You asked me that before.

(HE *doesn't answer.*)

(Finally) I didn't want it to happen.

HE. And was it true about your being desperate?

SHE. The novelty drove out the despair.

(Pause.)

HE. One Sunday afternoon, you weren't there, I don't remember now where you'd gone...I went for a walk through the town and I met a girl, a foreign girl just passing through...We went to a hotel. *(Pause)* It was marvellous. I didn't love her, I never saw her again. It was marvellous. Simple.

SHE. Was it necessary?

HE. No, why? It was marvellous but it wasn't necessary. I loved you.

(SHE *moves away from him.*)

SHE. Have you any more questions to ask me?

(Suddenly the sleeping hotel is filled with the sound of a telephone ringing.

They do not move.

Noise of someone moving about in reception, then the voice of the OLD LADY.)

O.L. Hello! Who did you want to speak to? *(Pause)* Monsieur Nollet? Yes, he's in. *(Pause)* Hold the line, please. *(Pause. Calling softly to* MICHEL NOLLET) Are you there, Monsieur Nollet?

(She knows they are both there.)

O.L. *(Calling, a bit flustered)* Monsieur Nollet...

(HE *hesitates.*)

HE.   Yes, I'm here.

(HE *goes over to the telephone, trying to master his emotion. He looks at* ANNE-MARIE, *and goes on looking at her as he answers the telephone. His voice sounds almost natural.*)

W.V.   Were you asleep?

HE.   Yes.

W.V.   Forgive me. I couldn't prevent myself from ringing...I don't know why, it's idiotic, but I was anxious. What have you been doing?

HE.   I went to the cinema, then I went for a stroll...then I went to bed.

W.V.   All this divorce business is so painful...I was anxious. Do forgive me.

HE.   Don't go worrying now, there's no need, it's silly.

W.V.   *(After a pause she says what's really on her mind)* You know, Michel, you didn't have to go. The case could have been heard and decided in your absence. It wouldn't have made any difference. *(Pause)* Are you there?

HE.   Yes.

(ANNE-MARIE *has come a few steps nearer.* HE *still looks at her as the voice on the telephone goes on.*)

W.V.   I don't want to be a nuisance, Michel, but the thought suddenly struck me...and I can't get rid of it...that's why I rang...to ask you why you went...

Say something, Michel...

(HE *doesn't answer.* ANNE-MARIE *looks at him as though it were she who had to answer. They both try to think of what to say to the woman at the other end of the line.*)

W.V.   Say something or I shan't be able to sleep. Michel... Michel...

HE.   To see her again.

(Silence at the other end. Then the voice resumes.)

W.V.   I knew. *(Pause)* Well?

(ANNE-MARIE says: 'Nothing'. And HE *replies in the same tone.)*

HE. Nothing.

(Pause.)

W.V. Are you sure?

HE. Yes. *(Pause)* Go to sleep now and stop worrying.

W.V. Are you quite sure?

HE. Yes.

(Pause.)

W.V. Will you still be coming back tomorrow?

HE. (HE *doesn't reply at once)* Of course.

(We don't hear the rest of what the voice at the other end says, just MICHEL NOLLET's *reply.)*

Goodnight, sleep well.

(HE looks at ANNE-MARIE *as he speaks. He puts down the receiver. Complete anti-climax and depression. Everything terrifyingly upside down. She is still standing, some distance away from him.)*

You said had I any questions to ask you.

SHE. Well...yes.

HE. *(Pugnaciously)* I couldn't bear you to be unfaithful and all the time I was unfaithful myself. Did you know?

SHE. Yes. Valèrie used to tell me about your... adventures.

HE. *(As before)* Didn't you think it was very unfair?

SHE. No, not unfair.

HE. What then?

SHE. Different. Difficult at first and then more and more...easy...understandable...I couldn't tell you, you wouldn't have accepted it.

HE *(Is this the real confession?)* You know...I still can't bear the idea that you didn't want it to happen.

(SHE doesn't answer. Silence.)

Did you hear?

SHE. Yes.

HE. What I really came for was to ask you what it was like.

(HE *laughs.*)

SHE. The same.

HE. Marvellous.

SHE. Yes. Remember. It was the same.

(And once again the telephone starts to ring. Their first impulse is to try to get away, then they stand motionless. We should get the impression that they are hunted, that they cannot go back without once more causing suffering and despair somewhere, and that they are aware of this.)

O.L. Madame Roche? Just a moment...*(To* MICHEL NOLLET)* Monsieur Nollet...there's someone asking to speak to Madame Roche...They say it's urgent... *(She stammers and stutters)*

HE. *(After looking at* ANNE-MARIE)* She's here. (ANNE-MARIE ROCHE *picks up the receiver.)*

MAN'S VOICE. Anita?

SHE. Yes.

M.V. Forgive me, Anita, I was anxious. It's nothing, just an idiotic anxiety...

(Pause)

SHE. Where are you?

M.V. On the way there, in a lorry-drivers' café, depressing place...There's still about another hundred kilometers...I won't wake you up again...don't worry... Anita...

(HE *listens to the conversation, completely transfixed. He finds it very hard to bear what she managed to bear a little while ago.*

The conversation still goes on.)

M.V. I love you, Anita...I can't sleep I'm so...happy it's all over, this divorce business...you can't imagine...

(Silence. Suddenly SHE *cries out.)*

SHE. Jacques...

80

M.V. What is it?

SHE. *(Recovering)* Come.

    (Pause.)

M.V. I'll start now.

    (SHE *hangs up. Pause.)*

SHE. Remember what it was like with that girl, that foreign girl, remember everything exactly. It was the same.

HE. *(Slowly)* It's impossible.

SHE. What is?

HE. To accept that.

SHE. *(Not altogether sincere)* Was it so marvellous? Really?

HE. Yes. *(Pause)* Do you understand?

SHE. No.

HE. Do you regret anything?

SHE. No. *(Pause)* When you say you came to ask me what it was like...it's not true.

HE. Well...not entirely...I came to see you again too, but I knew it would be no use.

SHE. How right you were.

HE. I couldn't even be near you without suffering.

    (Pause.)

SHE. What can we do to make these...memories...less painful?

HE. Nothing now, I think. The only thing that could have done me any good would have been to kill you, and so...

    (They look at each other.)

    I've become just a murderer out of a job... (HE *laughs)* It's ridiculous.

SHE. Now we're divorced they wouldn't acquit you.

HE. I know. (HE *laughs)* And even if I'd like to kill you I shouldn't like to die for it.

    (HE *goes towards her.* SHE *draws back.)*

HE. Listen, before this other man comes we still have a little time...

SHE. *(Very low, misunderstanding)* An hour.

HE. Listen...Would you tell me everything that happened? Everything?

SHE. You want me to try to describe happiness?

HE. Yes. Miserable happiness.

SHE. No. You're making a mistake. You've forgotten the girl in Evreux, so how could you imagine what happened in Paris?

HE. You think I've forgotten?

SHE. *(Speaking for both of them)* Yes.

(Silence. SHE goes away from him, leans against the wall, almost as if hiding.)

SHE. *(With great pain but also with an inner joy)* It doesn't matter about our being together...now, whether we're together or apart...it isn't worth making them suffer.

HE. Don't go to America. *(This is the first time he addresses her as 'tu')*

(SHE doesn't answer.)

(Terrified) Don't go. Don't go...Or else I'll come and live where you are, do you hear? To hell with my work...I'll come and live in the same town, I'll make your life a misery...until...

SHE. *(Interrupting)* ...Until hell starts up all over again?

HE. *(Raised voice)* What do you care about hell? *(Pause)* You either...*(Pause)* You don't give a damn about hell either. *(Pause, entreating)* Stay in France. So that at least we can meet, even if it's only by chance...so that it isn't entirely impossible. Let us at least both be in the same country... Otherwise...it will be unbearable.

(SHE doesn't answer.)

(Suddenly desperate) We can arrange to meet somewhere in the provinces, out of the way, no-one will know... no-one will ever know.

(They are both filled with anger against things as they are, circumstances.)

82

SHE. No. *(She shakes her head)* No...no...to want it, do
it deliberately, no...If we are to meet again, let it be
as you were saying before, by chance, as it was
with them, with the girl, let's see how chance
manages things. *(Crying it out)* Never otherwise,
never again, never again except by chance...

HE. *(In despair, exhausted, astonished)* To chuck
everything away like this, just because of that trip
to Paris, when all the time you were coming back...

(Silence.)

SHE. He'll be here soon.

HE. I can't leave you.

SHE. We're parted now...never again except by chance.

HE. What if one of us were dying...

SHE. Not even then.

(Long pause. Their voices change.)

HE. I don't understand what's happening. *(Pause)* The
beginning and the end are all mixed up...what can
we do so that you and I...our story (HE *smiles)*...
don't just disappear...

(Silence.)

SHE. The answer is...nothing...do nothing...invent it.

HE. Let love go on growing secretly, in the dark.

SHE. Yes.

HE. Like people kept apart by force of circumstance?

SHE. Yes. Look at me, I'm the only woman now who
is forbidden to you.

(Pause.)

HE. My wife. *(Long pause)* Shall we see each other
again?

SHE. I don't know.

HE. But if ever, once again, you and I...

SHE. Then we shall probably die, as lovers do.

HE. What is happening?

SHE. When?

HE. Now. The beginning or the end?

SHE.   Who knows?

    (Pause.)

HE.   Go and wait for him outside.

SHE.   *(Meekly, making us think of other circumstances)*
Yes.

    *(HE takes her arm and leads her to the door of the
hotel. SHE is gone. He stands motionless in front
of the door. As if he were asleep where he stands.)*

CURTAIN

L'Amante Anglaise

L'AMANTE ANGLAISE was first produced at the Royal
Court Theatre, London, as THE LOVERS OF VIORNE,
with the following cast:

CLAIR	Peggy Ashcroft
PIERRE	Maurice Denham
INTERROGATOR	Gordon Jackson

PIERRE LANNES

*The play should be performed on a platform projecting
into a small auditorium with the safety-curtain down.
No sets or special costumes.*

RECORDING.   On April 8th 1966 a piece of a human
body was found in a railway truck in France.

In the next few days other pieces were found
throughout France and elsewhere. With the
exception of the head, which couldn't be traced,
the body was reconstructed in Paris. It was a
woman.

By analysing the railway intersections the Paris
Flying Squad, which was in charge of the opera-
tion, was able to show that whatever their
destination all the trains concerned passed through
one point: under the Montagne Pavée bridge at
Viorne in the district of Corbeil.

Invested by the police the commune of Viorne —
2,500 inhabitants, 75 Portuguese — soon yielded
up its anatomist: Claire Amelie Lannes, 51 years
old, no occupation, resident in Viorne for twenty
years, ever since her marriage to Pierre Lannes.

Confronted by the police she at once confessed to
the murder of her deaf and dumb cousin,
Marie-Thérèse Bousquet.

INTERROGATOR.   Before we start let me remind you
you're not obliged to answer questions and you're
free to leave whenever you wish.

(Gesture of assent from PIERRE)

Will you say who you are, please?

PIERRE.   My name's Pierre Lannes. I come from
Cahors. I'm fifty-seven. I work in the Ministry of
Finance.

INT.   You've lived in Viorne since 1944. Twenty-two
years.

PIERRE.   Yes. Apart from two years in Paris we've lived here ever since we were married.

INT.   You married Claire Bousquet in Cahors in 1942.

PIERRE.   Yes.

INT.   As no doubt you know, she told the police she did it alone and you didn't know anything about it.

PIERRE.   It's the truth.

INT.   You found out at the same time as the police?

PIERRE.   I found out when she confessed in the Balto Café on the evening of April 13th.

INT.   Was it her idea to go to the Balto?

PIERRE.   Yes. It was the first time we'd been since the murder. She told me to go on in front and she'd join me. When she came she'd got a case with her and said she was going to Cahors. That evening. She hadn't been to Cahors for twenty years.

(Pause.)

There was a plain-clothes detective in the cafe. We started to talk about the murder. About how it could have happened. Someone tried to be clever and said he knew it had been done in the forest fifty yards from the viaduct.

(Pause.)

INT.   Who?

PIERRE.   Me. *(Pause)* I don't know what came over me. *(Pause)* Then she went over to the detective and said no, it wasn't in the forest, it was in a cellar, at four o'clock in the morning.

INT.   And before that you had no suspicion of what had happened?

PIERRE.   No. None.

INT.   I'd like you to tell me how she explained her cousin's absence.

PIERRE.   She said: 'Marie-Thérèse went to Cahors first thing this morning.' This was about seven o'clock, when I got up.

INT.   Did you believe her?

PIERRE. I didn't believe it was the whole truth
but I thought it was part of it. I didn't think she
was lying.

INT. Did you always believe what she told you?

PIERRE. Yes. Everyone did. I thought she might have
lied to me once about her past, but I didn't
think she lied to me any more.

INT. Her past?

PIERRE. Before we met. That was a long time ago,
nothing to do with the murder.

INT. You weren't surprised your cousin had gone?

PIERRE. I was very surprised. But to tell the truth the
first thing I thought of was the house. What a mess
everything would get into while she was away. I
asked Claire more about it. She had a perfectly
convincing story. Marie- Thérèse had gone home
because she wanted to see her father before he
died and she'd be back in a few days.

INT. After a few days did you remind her?

PIERRE. Yes. And she said: 'We're just as well
without her. I've written and told her not to
come back.'

INT. And you still believed her?

PIERRE. I thought she was hiding something but I
still didn't think she was actually lying.

INT. But various possibilities must have crossed your
mind?

PIERRE. Yes. The most likely one was that Marie-
Thérèse had suddenly got fed up with us and didn't
like to say so.

INT. You knew Marie-Thérèse well. What other
explanations occurred to you?

PIERRE. I thought she might have gone off with a man.
A Portuguese. It was all one to them if she was
deaf and dumb. They can't speak French.

INT. Might she have gone with Alfonso?

PIERRE. No. No, even before, there was no question
of feeling between her and Alfonso. It was just a
matter of convenience if you see what I mean.
One thing that never crossed my mind was that

Claire and Marie-Thérèse might have quarrelled.

INT.   What did you decide to do?

PIERRE.   Have Claire put in a home and go to Cahors after Marie-Thérèse. Then I'd have been able to tell her I was on my own and there wouldn't be so much work.

INT.   In other words her going was a good opportunity for you to get away from Claire?

PIERRE.   Yes. Not easy, but still. A godsend really.

INT.   And what if Marie-Thérèse wouldn't come back even though Claire had gone? Did you think of that?

PIERRE.   Yes. I'd have got someone else. I can't keep house for myself.

INT.   But you'd still have got rid of Claire?

PIERRE.   Yes. All the more reason. Someone new couldn't have put up with her in the house.

INT.   And it was because of all this you didn't try to find out any more about why Marie-Thérèse had gone?

PIERRE.   Partly. Partly because I hardly saw Claire those few days. It was fine and she was always out in the garden. I did the shopping on my way home from work.

INT.   Didn't she eat?

PIERRE.   No. I think she must have had something in the night. One morning there wasn't as much bread as there should have been.

INT.   Was she very tired during those five days?

PIERRE.   When I went to work she was in the garden. When I came back she was still there. She didn't see me. I'd become a complete stranger. I don't think she was tired. I'm talking now about after the murder. One day while it was all going on, if I remember rightly — that's right, one day I found her asleep on the bench in the garden. She looked exhausted, half dead. Next day I found her all dressed up at two in the afternoon. She said she was going to Paris. She didn't get back till late. About ten.

INT. She didn't go to Paris often?

PIERRE. Not in the last few years. Apart from that trip, whether it was during the crime or after, she must have spent all her time in the garden.

INT. Apparently she always spent a good deal of time there. So what was new?

PIERRE. Nothing, really. Just that without Marie-Thérèse there were no fixed times for anything, so she could stay out there as long as she liked. Till it was dark.

INT. Didn't you call her in?

PIERRE. I didn't feel like it any more. I'd been a bit scared of her for some time. Ever since she chucked the transistor down the well. I thought this must be the end.

INT. You weren't suspicious as well as scared?

PIERRE. Perhaps. But not about what had happened. How could I have been?

INT. Have you seen her since she was arrested?

PIERRE. Yes, I went to the prison the next day and they let me see her.

INT. What impression does she make on you now?

PIERRE. I don't understand anything any more. Even about myself.

INT. What were you afraid might happen?

PIERRE. With Marie-Thérèse not there, anything.

INT. She used to keep an eye on her?

PIERRE. Yes, she had to. Nothing rough, don't worry. Only I was afraid she'd create a scandal, or do herself in...

INT. You didn't go down to the cellar during that time?

PIERRE. I do go down in the winter for wood. But it was so warm we'd stopped having fires. Besides, she said: 'Don't bother going down to the cellar. Marie-Thérèse has taken the key with her.'

INT. You were afraid she'd kill herself? Or you hoped she would?

PIERRE. I don't remember.

INT. I'd like to know what you think: did she do it on her own or did someone help her?

PIERRE. On her own, I'm sure.

INT. Apparently she says she met Alfonso about two o'clock one morning when she was on her way to the viaduct with the shopping-bag.

PIERRE. In that case I don't know. Did they question Alfonso before he went?

INT. Yes. He denied having seen her since the murder. But he said that for years he often used to come across her in the village at night.

PIERRE. Really? That's impossible.

INT. Unless Alfonso's not telling the truth?

PIERRE. No. If he said it it's true.

INT. What did she use to say about Alfonso?

PIERRE. She never talked about him. She never talked about anyone. But when he came to chop wood she was pleased. She used to say: 'Thank God for Alfonso.'

INT. As you know, I'm not interested in the facts but in what lies behind them. What matters is what you think about her.

PIERRE. I see.

INT. Why do you think she said she'd met Alfonso?

PIERRE. She was very fond of him, so normally you'd expect her not to say anything in case it got him into trouble. I don't know.

INT. On the 13th of April, that evening in the Balto, you said — in front of the detective — that Alfonso knew all about the murder.

PIERRE. I'm not going to answer. *(Pause)* How do you know?

INT. The detective had a tape-recorder in his brief-case. The whole evening was recorded.

PIERRE. So you know everything?

INT. No. A tape only repeats what it remembers. It doesn't tell anything. But if anyone in Viorne was likely to know, who was it?

PIERRE. Him.

INT. Alfonso?

PIERRE. *(Doesn't answer)* Does she know he's left the country?

INT. No. I'm trying to find out what sort of a woman Claire Lannes is and why she says she committed this murder. She doesn't give any reason herself. So I'm trying to find out for her. Do you understand why she was fond of Alfonso?

PIERRE. He lived right away in a hut in the woods. He did odd jobs. That was how we came to know him. In Viorne they say he was a bit simple. *He* didn't talk much either. She must have made up things about him.

INT. Weren't they rather alike?

PIERRE. Perhaps, when you get right down to it. But she was sharper than he was.

What do people say about her? Have you asked?

INT. Now they say what people always say. That she was bound to break out sooner or later. I don't know what they said before. But no-one says you weren't happy with her.

PIERRE. I've always hidden the truth.

INT. About what?

PIERRE. The life I led with her. Nothing but total indifference for years.

She didn't look at us any more. At meals she sat without raising her eyes. It was as if she was frightened. As if as time went by she knew us less and less. Sometimes I thought it might be having Marie-Thérèse there that got her into the habit of not talking. Sometimes I was even sorry I'd brought her. But what else could I do? *She* never did anything. As soon as meals were over she'd go back into the garden, or else to her room, depending on the weather.

INT. What did she do in her room or in the garden?

PIERRE. If you ask me she just slept.

INT. Didn't you ever go and see her? Talk to her?

PIERRE.   No. You'd have to have lived with her to understand. Of course every so often I had to talk to her. I made a point of telling her about any major expense or when anything needed doing to the house. She always agreed to everything. Especially repairs to the house. She loved having a workman in. She'd follow him about everywhere and watch him working. Sometimes   it was a bit embarrassing for them, at least the first day. After that they didn't take any notice. It was really like having a sort of madwoman in the house. But harmless. That was why we weren't as careful as we ought to have been. Yes, that must be it. No need to look for any other explanation.

You know, it's got to the point where I've wondered if she didn't make it all up. If it really was her that killed the poor girl... But the fingerprints are the same? Aren't they?

INT.   I know nothing about it.

PIERRE.   Where could she have got the strength? If it weren't for the evidence could you believe it yourself?

INT.   No-one could. Perhaps she couldn't either. She says she once asked you if you'd ever dreamed you were committing a murder. She didn't say when it was. Do you remember?

PIERRE.   The examining magistrate's already asked me that. It was two or three years ago, I think. One morning. I have a vague recollection she said something about dreaming of a murder. I must have said it happened to everyone, me included.

INT.   And was that true?

PIERRE.   Yes. There was one time especially. A nightmare.

INT.   When?

PIERRE.   Not long before she asked me, I think. I pressed a button, there was an explosion, and...

INT.   Who was killed?

PIERRE.   ...

INT.   You don't have to answer, you know.

PIERRE. I know. But I'll have to some time. It was Marie-Thérèse Bousquet. But at the same time, in the nightmare, I was crying because I'd got the wrong person. I didn't really know who was supposed to die but I knew it wasn't Marie-Thérèse. I don't think it was my wife either.

INT. Haven't you tried to remember?

PIERRE. Yes. But I couldn't.

It's got nothing to do with what's happened. Why do you keep on about it?

INT. You don't have to answer.

So you both killed the same person. You in dream, she in reality.

PIERRE. But *I knew* I'd made a mistake.

INT. You can't have known in the dream itself. You must have seen, and put it right, just after.

PIERRE. How?

INT. In another dream. It must have been in the second dream you cried.

PIERRE. Maybe. I can't help what I dream.

INT. Of course not. Besides, you in dream, she in reality — you weren't both committing the same crime through Marie-Thérèse. Your real victims must have been different. Did you tell your wife about this dream? In detail, I mean?

PIERRE. I should think not.

INT. Why?

PIERRE. I never told her things like that. If I spoke about it at all it was just to keep her quiet, because she asked.

She hadn't any tact, she didn't realise there are some things you don't repeat. If I'd told her my dream about Marie Thérèse she was quite capable of talking about it at the table right in front of the poor thing.

INT. I thought she couldn't hear?

PIERRE. She could lip-read. She didn't miss anything you said. Whereas with my wife it took ages to tell her the simplest thing. Hours. And by the next

95

day she'd have forgotten it all.

I was very lonely with her.

INT.   Did she forget everything like that?

PIERRE.   No, I was over-simplifying... She had her own
sort of memory. Cahors, for instance. She remembered Cahors as if she'd only left it yesterday.
Yes, she remembered that all right.

INT.   Were you often unfaithful to her?

PIERRE.   Any man would have been. I'd have gone
mad if I hadn't. She must have known. She didn't
care.

INT.   What about her?

PIERRE.   I don't think she was ever unfaithful to me.
Not out of fidelity but because everything was all
the same to her. Even at the beginning, when we...
I had the feeling someone else would have served
the purpose just as well as me.

INT.   So she might easily have gone from one man to
another?

PIERRE.   Yes. But she could just as easily stay with
the same one. I happened to be there.

INT.   Can you give me an example of the sort of thing
she couldn't understand?

PIERRE.   Anything to do with the imagination. A
story or a play on the radio — you could never
make her see it hadn't actually happened. She was
a child in some ways.

She could understand television. After her own
fashion, of course. But at least she didn't ask
questions.

INT.   Did she read the paper?

PIERRE.   She said she did, but I'm not sure. She'd
read the headlines and then leave it. I'd say she
didn't read the paper.

INT.   She just pretended to?

PIERRE.   No. She never pretended about anything.
Not she. She thought she read the paper. That's
different. Once — it must be a good ten years
ago — she suddenly had a craze for reading. You

96

know — those rubbishy children's comics. I
don't know where she got them. It got on my
nerves. I told her she wasn't to read them. When
she still did I tore them up. After that she didn't
read anything.

I suppose it was my fault she didn't read any
more. Because of the business about the comics.
But it was for her own good. It's sad though.
Poor woman.

INT. Who?

PIERRE. Claire. My wife. Once, it must have been
about the same time as the comics, I made her
read aloud to me, a bit every evening, out of a
travel book. Amusing as well as instructive. But it
was no good. I gave up. Half that book is all the
serious reading she's done in her life.

INT. Didn't it interest her?

PIERRE. The thing was, she didn't see the point of
learning. Didn't know how to. While the book
was describing one country she'd be forgetting
the one from the night before. I just let it go. No
use keeping on at someone who doesn't want to
alter.

INT. What education did you have?

PIERRE. I got the first part of the baccalaureat. Then
my father died and I had to leave school. But
I've always tried to keep up with things. I like
reading.

INT. Would you say she was quite unintelligent?

PIERRE. No, I wouldn't. Sometimes she'd come out
with a remark on someone that would quite
astonish you. And when she was in one of her
moods she could be very funny. She and Marie-
Thérèse used to play the fool together sometimes.
That was at the beginning, when Marie-Thérèse
had just come. And sometimes she'd talk very
strangely, as if she was reciting something out of
a book.

I can remember something about the flowers in the
garden. She used to say: 'English mint is black
and smells of fish and comes from the Ile des
Sables.'

INT.   What would you have done if you'd been able to stay on at school?

PIERRE.   I'd have liked to go into industry.

INT.   You said she had no imagination. Or have I misunderstood?

PIERRE.   You've misunderstood. She couldn't understand what other people imagined. But she'd got a very powerful imagination herself. It must have occupied the most important place with her.

INT.   And didn't you know anything about what went on in it?

PIERRE.   Practically nothing... All I can tell you is that the things she made up might really have happened. They started off from something true, she didn't invent it all. For instance, sometimes she'd go on at me for reproaching her about things I'd never mentioned. But they were things I *might* have mentioned. It was as if she'd seen into my mind.

Then she'd tell us about conversations she'd had with people in the street. No-one would have believed she invented them.

INT.   You don't think she was unhappy about getting old?

PIERRE.   Not at all. That was the best thing about her. Quite a comfort sometimes.

INT.   How did you know?

PIERRE.   I knew.

INT.   What's your opinion about it?

PIERRE.   About whether or not she was intelligent, you mean?

INT.   Yes, if you like.

PIERRE.   Nothing stayed with her. It was impossible for her to learn anything at all. She could have studied if she'd wanted to. But it was as if she was closed to everything and open to everything, both at once. Nothing stayed with her, she retained nothing. Like a place without doors, that the wind sweeps through.

INT.   Would it be correct to say she had no curiosity?

PIERRE. No, that wouldn't be right either. But it was
curiosity of a peculiar kind. I think she was
interested in Marie-Thérèse for quite a while.
Especially at the beginning. She used to wonder
how she managed to live. She wondered that
about Alfonso too.

INT. Did she become them, Alfonso and Marie-Thérèse?

PIERRE. Almost. She'd chop wood for two days like
Alfonso. Or put wax in her ears and make signs like
Marie-Thérèse. You should have seen her. It was
almost unbearable.

INT. Could it have been that she saw other people as
empty and incomplete, and she wanted to fill
and complete them with what she made up?

PIERRE. I see what you mean. But it was more the
opposite. Other people must have seemed to her
impossible to know through the usual means —
conversation, feeling.

That was why I first fell in love with her. I've
thought about it a lot and I'm sure of it. And
when I turned to other women it was for the
same reason: she didn't need me. It was as if once
she knew me she could do without me.

INT. What was she full of, then? Say the first word
that comes into your head.

PIERRE. I don't know. I can't. Herself?

INT. But who was that?

PIERRE. I don't know.

INT. Do you find talking about her boring or interesting?

PIERRE. Interesting. More than I'd have expected.

INT. And talking about yourself?

PIERRE. That's interesting too.

INT. She never wrote letters, did she?

PIERRE. She used to write to the papers at one time. But
I don't think she's done it for ten years now. No.
She must almost have forgotten how to write.
Besides, she had nobody left in Cahors but her
uncle, Marie-Thérèse's father. Who would she have
written to?

INT. The man in Cahors? The policeman?

PIERRE: How do you know about him?

INT.   She mentioned him to the examining magistrate.

PIERRE.   No, I don't think she wrote to him. If you
know her you can't imagine her sitting down
and writing someone her news and asking them
for theirs. Any more than you can imagine her
reading. When she wrote to the papers she could
just put down anything that came into her head.

INT.   Did she ever see the policeman again after you
were married?

PIERRE.   As far as I know, no. Never. She'd been
very unhappy with him. I think she wanted to
forget him.

INT.   When?

PIERRE.   When she met me.

INT.   Was it to forget him that she got married?

PIERRE.   I don't know.

INT.   Why did you marry her?

PIERRE.   I was very attracted to her physically.
Mad about her. That probably made me blind to
all the rest.

INT.   The rest?

PIERRE.   Her strange character. Her madness.

INT.   Do you think you succeeded in making her
forget the policeman in Cahors?

PIERRE.   I don't think so. It was time did it in the
end. Not me. Even if it was me I didn't take his
place.

INT.   She never talked to you about him?

PIERRE.   Never. But I knew she thought about
him,' especially at first. But at the same time I
knew she wanted to forget him. When Marie-
Thérèse came she never even tried to find out
how he was. It was because of him we never
went there for the holidays. I'd been told he was
trying to find out her address, and I wasn't
taking any risks.

INT.   You were anxious not to lose her, then?

PIERRE.   Yes. In spite of everything. Even after the
beginning.

INT.   You never spoke to her yourself about the
policeman in Cahors?

PIERRE.   No.

INT.   Had she asked you not to?

PIERRE.   No. But what was the point? Just to have
her tell me she still loved him.

INT.   You're the sort of person who prefers not to
talk about things that hurt you?

PIERRE.   Yes, I am.

INT.   You knew she'd tried to kill herself because of
him? Thrown herself in a pond?

PIERRE.   I heard about it two years after we were
married.

INT.   How?

PIERRE.   I was active in politics in those days.
I hoped to be a candidate in the local elections.
My memory of it's all mixed up with politics,
because the chap who told me was a member
of the same group. He came from Cahors and
had heard about it by chance. But in the
party they didn't go in much for private
conversation. We soon moved on to another
subject.

INT.   You didn't speak to her about it?

PIERRE.   No.

INT.   And it didn't change your attitude towards
her?

PIERRE.   It did. How could I help feeling differently?
I knew she wouldn't have killed herself if I'd left
her.

INT.   Before you heard about it would you have thought
her capable of suicide?

PIERRE.   I wasn't all that surprised when I heard. So
I suppose I must have thought her capable of
it. But what she's done now — no, of course
not.

INT. Are you sure?

PIERRE. ...

INT. Why have you never left her?

PIERRE. She didn't look after the house properly
but Marie-Thérèse soon came so that wasn't a
problem any more. *(Pause)* These last few days
I've been thinking about what our life was like.
There was a time when I still loved her too much
to leave her. Even though her indifference made
me suffer. Later on, when I had other women, I
found her indifference attractive instead of
hurtful. She could still be very winning sometimes. As if she was visiting. Later on all that was
completely finished.

INT. You each kept your property separate when you
married.

PIERRE. Yes. That was my idea. She had an income
from a house in Cahors.

INT. Were you afraid of what she'd do if you left
her?

PIERRE. No. She'd probably have gone back to
Cahors. There'd have been nothing to be afraid
of.

INT. And there was never any question of a divorce?

PIERRE. No. I never mentioned it.

Perhaps I never met another woman I loved
enough to leave her. I thought I had once or
twice. But now I know I've never yet loved any
woman as I loved her.

INT. She doesn't know that?

PIERRE. No.

INT. Did you know about the other man before you
married her?

PIERRE. Yes. It was she told me. I decided to let
bygones be bygones. You can't prevent a woman
of thirty from having a past. And besides, I
wanted her to belong to me. I'd have done
anything.

INT. You didn't have to *marry* her.

PIERRE. That never occurred to me.

102

INT. When you look back over it all do you regret
marrying her?

PIERRE. I regret everything I've done.

INT. But her more than the rest?

PIERRE. I've had moments of personal happiness
with her that I can't regret.

It's only her that interests you in all I tell you,
isn't it?

INT. Yes.

PIERRE. Because of this murder?

INT. Well, it's because of the murder I've come to
be interested in her.

PIERRE. Because she's mad?

INT. More because she's someone who's never come
to terms with life.

PIERRE. Leave her in peace, can't you? It's pointless.
Just words. What's done can't be undone.

INT. What you've just said: 'Just words. What's done
can't be undone'—those are habitual expressions
with you, aren't they?

PIERRE. Yes, I suppose so. I spoke from habit. Like
the fool I am.

INT. Why do you say that? It was just automatic,
like what you said before.

PIERRE. Yes, I suppose it was.

INT. I imagine she never speaks like that?

PIERRE. No. She never makes remarks about life.

Are you learning anything about her from all
this?

INT. Are you?

PIERRE. ...

INT. I don't understand why you stayed with her
twenty-two years.

PIERRE. With her I was free. She's never asked me
a single question. I'd never have had such freedom
with anyone else. Anyone. I know they're not
very dazzling reasons but it's the truth. I used to
think that if I'd been unfaithful to her, that I'd

103

loved so much, I'd have been even more unfaithful to the others. Only it wouldn't have been nearly so easy. And then for a long time she was still attractive to me. There was nothing I could do about it. Once, in that political group I told you about, I met a woman I'd have liked to live with. She was free. She waited two years for me.

I used to tell Claire I had to go away on business, but I was really with her. Once we went to the Côte d'Azure—Nice. For a fortnight. It was agreed that after that I'd make up my mind whether to leave Claire or break with the other. I broke with the other.

INT.   Why?

PIERRE.   Perhaps because she was jealous. She used all I'd told her about Claire to run her down. I disliked her for that.

INT.   You weren't ever tempted...there wasn't ever anything between you and Marie-Thérèse Bousquet?

PIERRE.   You could say it crossed my mind sometimes, but no more than that. I'm not one to go in for that sort of thing.

INT.   That sort of thing...?

PIERRE.   Someone who worked in my house. And my wife's cousin into the bargain.

Marie-Thérèse herself wasn't one to make difficulties, as I suppose you've been told?

INT.   I've been told she was often seen in the forest in the evening with various Portuguese. But she never had a real affair with anyone?

PIERRE.   No. How could she? Deaf and dumb like that.

INT.   If you were asked what part you'd played in Claire Bousquet's life, what would you say?

PIERRE.   I've never asked myself the question.

INT.   *(Slowly)* It's a fairly meaningless question. But one could try to give an answer.

PIERRE.   I don't see what part I've played in her life.

INT.   What would have happened to her if you hadn't married her?

PIERRE.   Someone else would have married her. Her life would have been the same. She would have taken the heart out of any man as she did out of me. They'd probably have left her. But she'd have found others. That I'm sure of.

You remember my saying she lied about her past?

INT.   Yes.

PIERRE.   It was about that. All the lovers she'd had before we met.

INT.   Just after she tried to kill herself?

PIERRE.   Yes. For two years. I found out after we were married.

INT.   Did she actually lie to you? Or just not say anything about it?

PIERRE.   Just didn't say anything about it, though the normal thing would have been to tell me. And later on, when I asked her about it, she denied it. Why? Don't ask me.

INT.   So in fact you did talk to her about her past?

PIERRE.   Just that once. A few weeks after we were married.

INT.   Never again?

PIERRE.   No.

If no-one had married her she'd have gone on sleeping with Tom, Dick and Harry until she was old. So what? I've nothing against whores or women who sleep around. She'd have been just as well off.

INT.   The neighbours and the tradespeople say that as far as they know you never quarrelled.

PIERRE.   No, never. Not even that.

What else do they say?

INT.   They say, as you did, that you had affairs with other women. Even women in Viorne. And that your wife knew and didn't mind.

What did she do in the house after Marie-Thérèse came?

PIERRE.   Less and less every year.

INT.   But what?

PIERRE.   She did her own bedroom. Nowhere else.
She's always done that, every day. Thoroughly.
Too thoroughly.

She spent a long time getting dressed. At least an
hour every morning.

For years she used to go out a lot. In Viorne or
Paris. She used to go to Paris to the cinema. Or
she'd go and watch Alfonso chopping wood. She
watched television. She used to wash her own
things. She wouldn't let Marie-Thérèse touch
them. Who knows what else she did? She'd be
out in the garden, but doing what? For years, as
soon as it was spring, she'd be out in the garden
on the bench. I know it sounds incredible, but
it's true.

INT.   Marie-Thérèse was a good cook?

PIERRE.   Excellent, in my opinion.

INT.   The best you've come across?

PIERRE.   Yes. I often ate out, so I could compare.
I always ate best in my own house.

INT.   Did your wife like her cousin's cooking?

PIERRE.   Yes, I think so. She never said anything
about it.

INT.   Nothing at all? Are you sure?

(Pause)

PIERRE.   Sure. Why?

INT.   Didn't Marie-Thérèse ever take a holiday?

PIERRE.   You mustn't get it wrong. She wasn't a
servant. If she'd wanted to go away for a fortnight
she could have done.

INT.   But she never went?

PIERRE.   No, never. She was the real mistress of the
house.

INT.   So for twenty-one years Claire, your wife, ate
Marie-Thérèse Bousquet's cooking?

106

PIERRE. *(Surprised)* Yes. Why?

It was excellent. Well balanced. Plenty of variety.

INT. And the two women never quarrelled?

PIERRE. No. Of course I can't swear to it. I was out all day. Sometimes away for several days running. But I don't think they ever quarrelled.

INT. Think hard.

PIERRE. I am.

No, I can't remember anything.

INT. How did Claire speak of her?

PIERRE. Just normally. Once she called me and made me look at her from the kitchen door. She was laughing. She said: 'Look, from behind she's just like a calf.' We laughed, but not unkindly. It was true.

Sometimes, in the winter, I'd come home and find them playing cards together. No, they got on quite well.

INT. It's unusual for people who live together to get on so well.

PIERRE. I know. It would have been better if it had been different.

INT. Do you really think so?

PIERRE. Yes. Perhaps I was lulled into a false sense of security. If I was ever away I couldn't sleep. People seemed to talk too much. I feel as if I'd just woken up.

INT. You said a little while ago that Marie-Thérèse kept on eye on Claire. Nothing rough, you said.

PIERRE. Yes, she did, especially recently. It was necessary. Claire sometimes did...silly things. Risky things. Marie-Thérèse would tell me and I'd send her up to her room or out in the garden. It was best to leave her on her own.

INT. Who sent her to her room when you weren't there?

PIERRE. Marie-Thérèse.

INT. And that didn't disturb the peace?

PIERRE. It would have been more likely to disturb the

107

peace if we'd let her do just as she liked.

INT.   What, for instance?

PIERRE.   She'd put all the newspapers on the fire at
once. She broke things, plates mostly. She hid
things, or buried them. She said she'd lost her
watch and her wedding-ring, but I'm sure they're
in the garden. She used to cut things up too. Once
she cut up her blankets. But all you had to do was
be careful not to leave matches or scissors lying
about.

INT.   What about when Marie-Thérèse was out?

PIERRE.   We never left her alone in the house. And
we kept our rooms locked. Otherwise she'd have
been poking about everywhere.

INT.   Looking for what?

PIERRE.   That was really crazy. To find what she called
'particular traces' that had to be got rid of.

INT.   Everything was left unlocked at night?

PIERRE.   I have a feeling that Marie-Thérèse used to
lock the kitchen sometimes. When she spent the
night with one of her Portuguese perhaps.

INT.   Did she have them in her room?

PIERRE.   Probably, sometimes. Once I was up in my
room I didn't bother about what was going on
downstairs. Marie-Thérèse was quite entitled to
entertain whoever she liked.

INT.   You didn't hear anything the night of the murder?

PIERRE.   My room was on the first floor. From there
you could hardly hear anything from downstairs.

INT.   You didn't hear anything?

PIERRE.   I heard what sounded like a door.

INT.   You didn't hear anything then.

(PIERRE *doesn't answer.*)

You've left the house?

PIERRE.   Yes. I've taken a room at the station hotel.

INT.   Have you been back to the Balto?

PIERRE.   No. I use the hotel bar.

INT. Why haven't you been back?

PIERRE. I want to break with the past. Even the good
things.

INT. What are you going to do? Have you thought about
it?

PIERRE. I'm going to sell the house. Go and live
somewhere else. In the South.

INT. Don't you like the idea?

You don't remember anything in recent years that
might have foreshadowed the murder?

PIERRE. Perhaps right up to the last minute she didn't
think she was going to kill her. Don't you think
that's possible?

(Pause.)

INT. She never asked you anything about the train
intersections?

PIERRE. No. Whatever people say she must have thought
of that at the last moment. She must have been
walking about Viorne in the dark with her shopping
bag, looking for somewhere, and come to the
Montagne Pavée Bridge just as a train went by.
And the idea suddenly came to her. I can see her
as plainly as if I were there.

INT. The head—have you any idea about that?

PIERRE. None. I looked in the garden just on the off-
chance. Nothing.

INT. What's your opinion about the motives?

PIERRE. I'd say it was madness.

What you ought to have done perhaps was question
the man, the policeman in Cahors. He's the only
one who could have said what she was like when
she was twenty. But he's dead.

INT. Does she know?

PIERRE. I don't think so.

INT. Was she unhappy?

PIERRE. No. She wasn't unhappy. What do you think?

INT. I don't think she was unhappy either.

PIERRE. I ought to tell you that when she threw the

transistor down the well I asked the doctor to
come and have a look at her. He was supposed
to have called this week.

INT.   She threw your glasses down the well too,
didn't she?

PIERRE.   Yes. Her own too.

INT.   How do you know?

PIERRE.   I saw her from my window. She must
have thrown the key to the cellar down as well.
It's never been found.

INT.   Why do you think she threw the glasses down
there?

PIERRE.   I did think it was to prevent me from
reading the paper. But now I think it was for
another reason.

INT.   So that the disaster should be complete?

PIERRE.   So that it should be...*shut away* is the
expression that occurs to me.

She'd dragged the television set into the hall
and put it against Marie-Thérèse's door with an
old skirt over it. I put it back in its proper
place. She didn't even notice. The next day
she was arrested.

INT.   Have you got any letters or anything with her
writing on? Even old ones?

PIERRE.   No. Nothing.

INT.   We haven't got a single sample of her writing.

PIERRE.   Two or three years ago I found drafts of
some of those letters she wrote to the papers
in Versailles. They were almost illegible and
full of mistakes. I threw them away.

INT.   What were they about?

PIERRE.   I only remember one. She was writing for
advice about English mint. How to look after
it indoors in winter. Instead of 'la menthe' she
put 'l'amante'. 'Lover'.

But did she write something on the body?

INT.   Yes. Always the same two words. On the
walls too. 'Alfonso' on one wall. And on the

110

other wall 'Cahors'. No mistakes.

PIERRE. *(Slowly)* Alfonso. Cahors.

INT. Yes.

PIERRE. Yes.

INT. Have you anything more to say about the murder?

PIERRE. It's very difficult to explain what I think.

I think that if Claire hadn't killed Marie Thérèse she'd have ended up killing someone else.

INT. You?

PIERRE. Yes. She was moving in the dark towards murder. It didn't matter who was at the end of the tunnel. Marie-Thérèse or me.

INT. What was the difference between you?

PIERRE. I would have heard her coming.

INT. Who ought she to have killed, according to the logic of her madness?

PIERRE. Me.

INT. You just said 'Marie-Thérèse or me'.

PIERRE. I've just realised the truth.

INT. Why you?

PIERRE. I know.

BLACKOUT

CLAIRE LANNES

Different tempo. Slower, with unexpected pauses from
CLAIRE.

INT. Claire Lannes, how long have you lived in Viorne?

CLAIRE. Ever since I left Cahors. Apart from two
  years in Paris.

INT. Ever since you married Pierre Lannes.

CLAIRE. That's right.

INT. You haven't any children?

CLAIRE. No.

INT. You've never had a job?

CLAIRE. No.

INT. You've confessed to the murder of your cousin
  Marie-Thérèse Bousquet.

CLAIRE. Yes.

INT. You also say you had no accomplice?

CLAIRE. ...

INT. You did it all by yourself?

CLAIRE. Yes.

INT. You still insist that your husband knew nothing
  about it?

CLAIRE. He never woke up. I don't know what you
  want.

INT. To talk to you.

CLAIRE. About the murder?

INT. Yes.

CLAIRE. Ah.

INT. We'll begin with those journeys to and fro at night between your house and the Montagne Pavée bridge. Is that all right?

CLAIRE. Yes.

INT. Did you ever meet anyone?

CLAIRE. Once I met Alfonso. He's a woodcutter who lives in Viorne.

INT. I know.

CLAIRE. He was sitting on a stone at the side of the road, smoking. We said good-evening.

INT. What time was it?

'CLAIRE. Between two and half-past in the morning, I think.

INT. He didn't seem surprised? Didn't ask you what you were doing there?

CLAIRE. No. He was there himself, wasn't he?

INT. What do you think he was doing?

CLAIRE. I don't know. Waiting for it to get light perhaps. I don't know anything about it.

INT. You don't think it strange that he didn't ask any questions?

CLAIRE. No.

INT. You weren't frightened when you saw him?

CLAIRE. No. Who are you? Another policeman?

INT. No.

CLAIRE. Do I have to answer you?

INT. Why, does it bother you?

CLAIRE. No. I'm quite willing to answer questions about the murder and about myself.

INT. You told the examining magistrate: 'One day Marie-Thérèse was in the kitchen...' And then you didn't finish the sentence. I'd like you to finish it for *me*.

CLAIRE. All right... She was getting the dinner. It was the evening. I went in the kitchen and looked at her from behind and saw she had a sort of mark on her neck. Just here.

114

What will they do to me?

INT. They don't know yet.

Is that all you have to say about that evening?

CLAIRE. When she was dead the mark was still there. On her neck. Then I remembered seeing it *before*.

INT. Why did you tell the examining magistrate about this?

CLAIRE. Because he asked me for dates. I was trying to sort it all out. I think there must have been several nights between the two times I noticed the mark.

INT. Why didn't you finish the sentence with the magistrate?

CLAIRE. Because it had nothing to do with the murder. I realised that in the middle of the sentence.

INT. Hadn't you ever seen the mark before?

CLAIRE. No. I only saw it because she'd done her hair. differently. It left her neck uncovered.

INT. Did it make her look different too?

CLAIRE. No. Not her face.

INT. Who was Marie-Thérèse Bousquet?

CLAIRE. She was my cousin. She'd been deaf and dumb from birth. She had to be found something to do. She was a big woman. Always happy.

Someone told me that because I'm a woman they'll only send me to prison for the rest of my life.

INT. Would you think that just or unjust?

CLAIRE. Just. And unjust.

INT. Why unjust?

CLAIRE. I don't know.

INT. Don't you think it's unjust to your husband? What you did, I mean?

CLAIRE. Not really. Better off alive than dead. And anyway...

INT. What? ·

CLAIRE. I wasn't all that fond of Pierre Lannes.

115

INT. Why did he arrange for Marie-Thérèse Bousquet to come?

CLAIRE. To help in the house. And it didn't cost anything.

INT. Not to do the cooking?

CLAIRE. No. When he arranged for her to come he didn't know she could cook. It was because it didn't cost anything. It was only afterwards he started to pay her something, I think.

INT. You keep saying you've told the police everything, but it isn't quite true.

CLAIRE. Are you questioning me to find out what I haven't told them?

INT. No. Do you believe me?

CLAIRE. Yes, all right. I've told everything except the head. When I tell about the head I'll have told everything.

INT. When will you tell about it?

CLAIRE. I don't know. I did what had to be done. It was a lot of trouble. I don't know if I shall tell.

INT. Why not?

CLAIRE. Why?

INT. They can't be quite sure it's her until the head's been found.

CLAIRE. Her hands would be enough. You'd easily recognise them. Ask my husband.

INT. If you don't want to say where you hid it, could you tell me when?

CLAIRE. I saw to the head last, one night. I'd been puzzling for a long time what to do with it. I couldn't think of anything. So I went in to Paris. I got off at the Porte d'Orléans and walked until I found what I wanted. I found it.

I don't understand what you want.

What did he say about me—my husband?

INT. He was quite nice. He said you'd changed. That you didn't talk much. One day you said Marie-Thérèse Bousquet was like an animal.

116

CLAIRE. I said 'a calf'. If you think it was because I said that that I killed her you're wrong. I'd have known.

INT. How?

CLAIRE. When the magistrate asked me about it.

INT. Did you ever dream you were somebody else?

CLAIRE. Of course not.

I dreamed about what I've just done. But a long time before. I told my husband. He said it had happened to him too. He said everyone dreamed about murder.

INT. Did you tell the magistrate it was as if you were dreaming when you killed Marie-Thérèse Bousquet?

CLAIRE. No. They asked me and I said it was worse.

INT. How?

CLAIRE. Because I wasn't dreaming.

What is it you want to find out?

INT. Why you killed Marie-Thérèse Bousquet.

CLAIRE. Why?

INT. I want to know.

CLAIRE. Is it your job?

INT. No.

CLAIRE. You don't do it every day? With everyone?

INT. No.

CLAIRE. Listen then. There are two things. The first is I dreamed I was killing her. The second is when I killed her I wasn't dreaming.

Is that what you wanted to know?

INT. No.

CLAIRE. If I knew how to answer you I would. But I can't sort out my ideas.

INT. But perhaps we'll manage it in the end?

CLAIRE. Perhaps.

If I did manage it what would they do to me?

INT. It would depend on your motives.

CLAIRE. I know that the more clearly criminals explain themselves the more they execute them.

What do you say to that?

INT. That in spite of the risk you want the whole truth to be known.

CLAIRE. I suppose you're right.

I ought to tell you I've dreamed I was killing all the people I've ever lived with including the policeman in Cahors, my first lover. Several times, each of them. So I was bound to do it. Really. Once.

INT. Your husband said you hadn't anything against Marie-Thérèse Bousquet. She did her work well. He never knew of any quarrel between you in twenty-one years.

CLAIRE. She was deaf and dumb. Nobody could have quarrelled with her.

INT. But if she hadn't been, would you have grumbled at her?

CLAIRE. How should I know?

INT. But you agree with what your husband said about her?

CLAIRE. The house belonged to her. I'd never have thought about whether she did her work well or badly.

INT. And now she's not there any more?

CLAIRE. I can see the difference. Dust everywhere.

INT. You prefer it like that?

CLAIRE. It's better clean, isn't it?

INT. But what do you really prefer?

CLAIRE. Cleanliness took up a lot of room. Too much.

INT. You mean it took the place of something else?

CLAIRE. Perhaps.

INT. What? Say the first word that occurs to you.

CLAIRE. Time?

INT. Cleanliness took the place of time. Is that it?

CLAIRE. Yes.

INT. And the delicious cooking?

CLAIRE. Worse still.

> Now the stove's cold. There's cold fat all over the tables and on top of that, dust. You can't see through the windows. Every ray of sunshine shows up the dust and grease. There's no clean crockery. Not a glass. Everything in the sideboard's been used.

INT. You say 'now'. But you're not there any more.

CLAIRE. I know what it's like.

INT. Like a garret?

CLAIRE. I don't understand.

INT. I mean as dirty as a garret.

CLAIRE. Why a garret?

INT. If it had gone on like that what would have happened?

CLAIRE. But it is going on. There's no-one there. It began while I was still there. No washing-up for a week.

INT. What will happen?

CLAIRE. Soon you won't be able to see anything. Grass will grow up between the tiles. Soon there won't be room to get in. It won't be a house, it'll be a pigsty.

INT. Or a garret?

CLAIRE. No. A pigsty. It had made a good start when I was arrested.

INT. Didn't you do **anything** to prevent it?

CLAIRE. No. Nothing one way or the other. We'll just see what happens.

INT. You were taking a holiday?

CLAIRE. When?

INT. Since the house started to get dirty?

CLAIRE. I never took a holiday. There was no need. My time was my own, my husband earns good money, and I've got an income from a house in Cahors. Didn't my husband tell you?

INT. Yes.

How do you find the prison food?

CLAIRE. You want me to say if it's all right?

INT. Yes.

CLAIRE. It's all right.

INT. Is it good?

CLAIRE. It's all right.

Am I saying what you want me to say?

INT. Yes.

CLAIRE. Tell them if they think they ought to put me in prison for the rest of my life, all right, let them get on with it.

INT. Do you miss anything from the life you used to live?

CLAIRE. I'm quite comfortable here. All my family are gone. It won't be too bad here.

INT. But isn't there anything you miss from the old life?

CLAIRE. What part?

INT. The last few years, say.

CLAIRE. Alfonso.

Alfonso and Cahors.

INT. Was she the last one of your family?

CLAIRE. Not quite. There's her father. Alfred Bousquet. All the Bousquets are dead now except her father. He only had the one daughter, Marie-Thérèse, deaf and dumb, what luck, it killed his wife.

I don't count my husband.

She was my own flesh and blood. We had the same name. They said she was very cheerful for someone deaf and dumb. More cheerful than a normal person.

INT. In spite of her infirmity you didn't think of her as different from yourself?

CLAIRE. Of course not. Not when she was dead.

INT. And alive?

CLAIRE. She was fat, she ate a lot, and she slept like a log every night.

INT. And that made more difference than her being deaf and dumb?

CLAIRE. Yes. Perhaps. When she ate, when she walked about, sometimes I couldn't bear it. I didn't tell the magistrate that.

INT. Can you try to explain why? Why you didn't tell him?

CLAIRE. He'd have misunderstood, he'd have thought I hated her, and I didn't hate her. I wasn't sure I could explain it to him so I didn't say anything. What I've just told you is to do with my character, that's all. All I'm saying is I'm a person who can't bear people eating and sleeping well. That's all. If it had been someone else, not her, eating and sleeping like that, I'd have found it just as unbearable. So it wasn't because it was her. It was because I couldn't stand it in anyone. Sometimes I used to get up from the table and go out in the garden. Sometimes I was sick. Especially when there was stew. Stew is something terrible for me. Terrible. I don't know why. And yet we often had it in Cahors when I was small. My mother made it because it was cheaper than just meat.

INT. Why did Marie-Thérèse make it if you didn't like it?

CLAIRE. No particular reason, just to make something, without thinking, she made it because my husband loves it, she made it for him, for herself, for me, for nothing.

INT. Didn't she know you didn't like it?

CLAIRE. I never told them.

INT. Couldn't they have guessed?

CLAIRE. No. If I didn't watch them eat it I could manage to eat it myself.

INT. Why didn't you ever tell her you hated it?

CLAIRE. I don't know.

INT. Think.

CLAIRE. I didn't think 'I don't like stew' so I

121

couldn't say it. Do you think it could be that?

INT.   It's only talking to me that you realise you could have told them?

CLAIRE.   Perhaps. I must have swallowed tons of it. I don't really understand.

INT.   Why didn't you just leave it?

CLAIRE.   In a way I didn't dislike eating that horrible greasy gravy.

Have I told you how fond I was of the garden? I was left in peace there. In the house I could never be sure she wouldn't suddenly come up and kiss me. I didn't like her kissing me. She was very fat and the rooms are small. She was too fat for the house.

INT.   Did you tell her?

CLAIRE.   No.

INT.   Why?

CLAIRE.   Because it was only for me, me, when I her in the house, that she was too fat. Otherwise no. But it wasn't only her. My husband's long and thin and I found him too tall for the house. Sometimes I used to go out in the garden so as not to see him with his head scraping the ceiling.

INT.   And they didn't come out in the garden after you?

CLAIRE.   No. There's a concrete bench and a bed of English mint. It's my favourite plant. You can eat it. It grows on islands where there are sheep. I sometimes felt very clever on that bench. I'd just sit there without moving, and I'd have very intelligent thoughts.

INT.   How did you know?

CLAIRE.   One knows.

Now I'm only the person you see in front of you.

INT.   And who were you in the garden?

CLAIRE.   The one that's left after I'm dead.

INT.   Did you do a lot of things you liked and disliked at the same time?

CLAIRE.   Some.

122

INT.   In what way did you like them?

CLAIRE.   I thought about them afterwards in the garden.

INT.   In the same way every day?

CLAIRE.   No, never.

INT.   Did you think about another house?

CLAIRE.   No, the one that was there.

INT.   But without them in it?

CLAIRE.   No, with them. They were there, right behind me in the house.

I tried to think of explanations, explanations that would never have occurred to *them,* right behind me in the house.

INT.   Explanations of what?

CLAIRE.   Oh, lots of things.

I don't know what I did with my life up to now. I loved the policeman in Cahors.

Who'll be any better off for my going to prison?

INT.   No-one and everyone. I don't know.

CLAIRE.   It's all one to me. Did my husband tell you about the policeman in Cahors?

INT.   Very little.

CLAIRE.   You see me now, but once I was twenty-five and he loved me. He was wonderful. I believed in God then and went to mass every day. He was living with another woman so at first I wouldn't have anything to do with him. We were madly in love for two years. Madly. It was he who took me away from God. After God, I saw everything only through him. He was the only one I listened to, he was everything to me, and one day God wasn't there any more, only him. Only him. And then one day he lied to me. The heavens fell.

(Silence. She is thinking of her attempted suicide.)

Three years afterwards I met Pierre Lannes. He took me to Paris. I didn't have any children. I wonder what I did with my life.

INT.   Did you never see the policeman from Cahors again?

CLAIRE.   Yes, once, in Paris. He came from Cahors to see me. He came to where I lived. My husband wasn't there. He took me to a hotel near the Gare de Lyon.

He wanted me to go back to him but it was too late.

INT.   How?

CLAIRE.   To love each other as we used to. I tore myself away from him. He couldn't let me go. We parted for ever in that room near the Gare de Lyon.

INT.   Had Marie-Thérèse Bousquet come to live with you yet when that happened?

CLAIRE.   No. She came the year after. My husband brought her from Cahors on March 8th 1945. She was nineteen. It was a Sunday morning. I saw them coming up the street. From a distance she looked like everyone else. Close to, she didn't speak.

The house was almost silent. Especially in winter, after the children went home from school.

In the winter I couldn't go out in the garden. I stayed in my room. Have you asked the people in Viorne about the murder?

INT.   They say they don't understand.

CLAIRE.   I forgot to take my last look at Viorne from the police van. You don't think of these things. What I can still see is the square at night, and Alfonso strolling up smoking, and smiling when I come.

INT.   Some people say you had everything to make you happy.

CLAIRE.   I had all the time in the world.

INT.   Others say they expected it.

CLAIRE.   Really?

INT.   Are you unhappy, at this moment?

CLAIRE.   No. I'm almost, I'm on the brink of being happy. If I had the garden I'd be over the brink and quite happy, but they'll never give it back to me and I prefer, I prefer that sorrow.

If I had my garden I wouldn't be able to bear it, it would be too much. No. What is it they say, then?

INT. That you had everything to make you happy.

CLAIRE. True.

In the garden I thought about happiness. I can't remember at all what I used to think on the bench. Now everything's finished I can't understand what I used to think.

INT. Why do you say 'Everything's finished'? Do you really think so?

CLAIRE. What could begin? So it's all finished.

Finished for her that's dead. Finished for me who did it.

Finished for the house. It went on for twenty-two years. Now it's finished.

Just one long, long day. Day, night. And the murder.

INT. What do you remember?

CLAIRE. The winter, when I couldn't go out in the garden. Apart from that it's all the same.

I believe I thought about everything, sitting on that bench.

People went by and I'd think about them. I thought about Marie-Thérèse, about how she managed. I put wax in my ears. Not often, perhaps about ten times, that's all. Did my husband say he was going to sell the house?

INT. I don't know.

CLAIRE. Oh, he'll sell it. And the furniture. What else can he do with it now? He'll have it auctioned in the street. People will come and see the beds out in the street. The beds in the street. They'll see the dust and the tables covered in grease and the dirty dishes. That's how it has to be.

Perhaps he'll have trouble selling the house because of the murder. He may only get the price of the land. It's worth about seven hundred francs per square metre now, so with the garden he shouldn't do so badly.

But what will he do with the money?

INT. Do you think you had everything to make you happy?

CLAIRE. Yes, from the point of view of those who say so and believe it. For other people, no.

INT. What other people?

CLAIRE. You.

INT. But according to you I'm wrong too, if I think you were unhappy?

CLAIRE. Yes. When I remember what it was like with the policeman in Cahors. I could say: nothing exists besides that. But that's not so. I've never been separated from the happiness in Cahors, it overflowed on to my whole life. It wasn't a happiness of a few years, don't think that, it was a happiness to last for ever. I always felt I'd like to tell someone about it, but who could I talk to about him?

I could have written letters about him, yes, but who to?

INT. Him?

CLAIRE. No, he wouldn't have understood.

No, they ought to have been written to just anyone. But it isn't easy to find just anyone.

I ought to have sent them to someone who didn't know either the policeman in Cahors or Claire Lannes, so that it could all be completely understood.

INT. To the papers perhaps?

CLAIRE. No. I did write to the papers two or three times for various reasons but never anything so serious.

INT. What came between the garden and the rest?

CLAIRE. The moment when the smell of cooking started. There was only an hour left till dinner, you had to think what you had to think quickly because you only had an hour left before the end of the world.

You see, monsieur, in the garden I had a lid made

126

of lead over my head. My thoughts would have had to get through it for...for me to have...

INT.   Peace?

CLAIRE.   Yes. But they hardly ever managed to get through. Mostly they just stayed there seething. It hurt so much that several times I thought of doing away with myself.

INT.   But sometimes they got through?

CLAIRE.   Sometimes, yes, they got out for a few days. I'm not mad, I know they weren't going anywhere. But when they were going through me to take flight, I was so...the happiness was so great I almost thought I'd gone mad. I thought people must hear, that my thoughts went off like pistol-shots.

Sometimes people turned round and looked at the garden as if they'd been called. I mean that's what it seemed like to me.

INT.   What were these thoughts to do with? Your life?

CLAIRE.   If they'd been to do with my life they wouldn't have made anyone turn round. No, they were about lots of other things. I had thoughts about happiness, and plants in winter, certain plants, certain things...

INT.   What?

CLAIRE.   Food, politics, water, thoughts about water, cold lakes, the beds of lakes, lakes on the beds of lakes, about water, thirsty water that opens and swallows up and closes again, lots of thoughts about water, about creatures that crawl for ever without hands, about what comes and goes, lots of thoughts about that too, about the idea of Cahors when I think about it and the idea of it when I don't, about television and how it gets mixed up with all the rest, one story upon another upon another, about seething, a lot about that, seething and seething, result: more seething and so on, about things being mixed up and things being separate, oh a lot about that, seething that's separate and seething that's not, you understand, each grain separate but stuck together too, seething multiplication and division, about the whole mess and all that's lost, and so on and so on, ask me another.

INT.   About Alfonso?

127

CLAIRE. Oh yes, a lot. He's without limits. Open heart. Open hands. Empty house. Empty case. And no-one to see he's perfect.

INT. About people who've committed murder?

CLAIRE. Yes, but I got it wrong, I realise that now. But I couldn't talk about that except to someone else who'd done it too and could help me. Not to you.

INT. Would you have liked other people to know about the thoughts you had in the garden?

CLAIRE. Yes.

I'd have liked to let them know I'd got answers for them. But how?

INT. By talking?

CLAIRE. No. I wasn't intelligent enough for the intelligence that was in me.

INT. You would have liked to be completely intelligent?

CLAIRE. Yes. Completely.

What consoles me for dying some day is not having been it completely.

I never managed it. I imagine it must be terrible to be very intelligent and know your intelligence must die the same as you.

INT. Let's get back to the murder. If you don't mind.

(Pause.)

CLAIRE. I hardly know anything about then. They must have told you.

INT. Why did you do it?

CLAIRE. What are you referring to?

INT. Why did you kill her?

CLAIRE. If I could have said you wouldn't be there asking me questions. I know about the rest.

INT. The rest?

CLAIRE. If I cut her up in pieces and threw the pieces into trains it was because it was a way of getting rid of her. Put yourself in my place. What would you have done?

128

Anyway they say it wasn't such a bad idea. I didn't want to be caught before I was ready, and I did get rid of her.

INT. And now that you have been caught?

CLAIRE. Oh, I suppose I'll go to jug. It's too tiring, all this butchery. Better to go to jug. They put some people to sleep right away.

INT. Who told you that?

CLAIRE. It's well known.

INT. You don't know why you killed her?

CLAIRE. I shan't tell.

INT. What will you tell?

CLAIRE. That depends on the question.

INT. You've never been asked the right question?

CLAIRE. No. If I had I'd have found an answer.

INT. Do you try to think of the right question your yourself?

CLAIRE. Yes, but I haven't found it. I don't try very hard.

They've paraded questions past me and I haven't recognised one.

INT. Not one...?

CLAIRE. No. They ask: Did she get on your nerves being deaf and dumb? or: Were you jealous of your husband? or: Were you unhappy?

At least you haven't asked me anything like that.

INT. What's wrong with those questions?

CLAIRE. They're separate.

INT. The right one would include all those and others as well?

CLAIRE. Perhaps.

You're interested to know why I did it?

INT. Yes. I'm interested in you. So everything you do interests me. What would you call a good question? I mean if *you* were asking *me?*

CLAIRE. Why should I do that?

INT. To find out why I'm questioning you, say.

129

In what way you interest me. What *I'm* like.

CLAIRE. I know in what way I interest you. And I already know a bit what you're like.

> With Alfonso, when he came to talk to Pierre about work or anything, I used to stand behind the door and listen. I'd have to do the same with you.

INT. I'd have to be talking at a distance?

CLAIRE. Yes, and to someone else.

INT. Without knowing you were listening?

CLAIRE. That's right. It would have to happen by chance.

INT. One can understand things better from behind doors?

CLAIRE. Everything. It's marvellous. Like that I've seen right into Alfonso, deeper than he can himself.

INT. What did Pierre sound like through the door?

CLAIRE. Him? The same as ever.

> Listen, I can't say fairer than this: if you find the right question I swear I'll answer it.

INT. And suppose there was a motive but it was unknowable? Unknown?

CLAIRE. Unknown to whom?

INT. Everyone. You. Me.

CLAIRE. Where?

INT. In you?

CLAIRE. Why? Why not in her, or in the house, or in the knife? Or in death? Yes, in death.

> Is madness a motive?

INT. Perhaps.

CLAIRE. When they get tired of trying they'll say it's madness. I know. Oh well.

INT. Don't think about it.

CLAIRE. It's you who's thinking about it. I can always tell when people think I'm mad by the sound of their voice.

INT. What did you do in the house?

CLAIRE. Nothing. The shopping every other day. Marie-Thérèse gave me a list.

INT. But you did something?

CLAIRE. No.

INT. But how did the time pass?

CLAIRE. At fifty miles an hour, like a torrent.

INT. Your husband said you did your room every day.

CLAIRE. To please myself I did my room and washed, myself and my things. Like that I was always ready, you see, and so was the room. Clean and tidy and the bed made. I could go into the garden and there'd be no trace left behind.

But if the other women are all mad what will happen to me?

INT. When you'd washed and the room was done, what was it you were ready for?

CLAIRE. Nothing. It was just ready. If things had happened, if someone had come for me, if I'd disappeared, if I'd never come back, they'd have found nothing left behind, not a single trace that was particular, only traces pure and simple.

INT. Tell me about the house. How were the rooms set out?

CLAIRE. Two bedrooms on the first floor and on the ground floor the dining-room and Marie-Thérèse's room.

INT. Had you been to sleep before you went down to her room?

CLAIRE. I didn't have to switch the light on so it couldn't have been still dark. So I must have been to sleep.

I often used to wake at dawn and walk about the house.

The sun was coming in between the dining-room and the passage.

INT. ...The door of her room was open and you saw her asleep on her side. With her back to you.

131

CLAIRE. Yes.

INT. You went into the kitchen for a drink. You looked round.

CLAIRE. *(Shouting)* Yes. Underneath the plates I can see what was written on the ones we bought in Cahors three days before the wedding. 'Bazar de l'Etoile 1942'. It's starting again. I know I'll be driven to thinking about the plates. About all that. And then I've had enough, you see. I want them to come and take me away. I want three or four walls, a steel door, an iron bed, a barred window, and Claire Lannes shut up inside. So I open the window and smash the plates so that they'll hear and come and clear me away. But suddenly she's standing there in the draught from the door. Looking at me.

INT. *(Referring to the murder)* When was it?

CLAIRE. When I smashed the plates? About three years ago. Perhaps five.

INT. How could your husband have believed you when you said Marie-Thérèse had gone to Cahors?

CLAIRE. Oh, let me alone a minute.

What is it you want to know?

INT. What did you tell your husband when he got up?

CLAIRE. I said what you just said. That she'd gone to Cahors.

He didn't believe me.

INT. Didn't he ask any questions?

CLAIRE. No.

INT. So what did he think had happened?

CLAIRE. I don't know.

INT. Do you think Alfonso guessed?

CLAIRE. When I asked him to throw the television down the well I saw he'd guessed.

Alfonso. He sings *La Traviata* on his way home sometimes. Apart from that he's always chopping wood. What a bore. Twelve years ago I hoped he might love me, Alfonso, and take me into the forest with him. But it will never happen, that

132

love. All night I waited for him, once. I listened for every sound. It would have been love again. Cahors, together.

INT.   Didn't he come?

CLAIRE.   I don't think so. No. Perhaps.

———————— OPTIONAL CUT ————————

They'll all say I'm mad now. Let them say what they like. They're on the other side, they'll say anything, without thinking.

INT.   Were you on the same side as they are before the murder?

CLAIRE.   No, never. I've never been on their side. If I ever had to go there, say when I did the shopping — I did the shopping every other day — I'd hear their voices echoing for an hour afterwards. Like in a theatre.

INT.   Did you go to the theatre?

CLAIRE.   Sometimes he took me when we lived in Paris.

La Traviata was in Cahors with the other.

Alfonso was on the same side as me, even if he didn't know it.

So was the policeman in Cahors. Both feet.

INT.   Do you know what became of him?

CLAIRE.   He's still shut away there, leading the life he likes, going from one woman to another.

INT.   Was your husband 'on the other side'?

CLAIRE.   Yes and no. He was cut out to be, but because of us he never quite went over. With a wife like me on one side and a deaf and dumb cousin on the other, he was stuck. Otherwise...

Where is he now?

INT.   At the hotel.

CLAIRE.   Really?

INT.   Was Marie-Thérèse Bousquet 'on the other side'?

CLAIRE.   Because of being deaf and dumb she wasn't anywhere. But if she'd been normal she'd have

133

been the queen of the other side. Mark my words —
the queen. They used to smile at her, so you see.
They never smiled at me.

──────────── END OF OPTIONAL CUT ────────────

(Wildly) She was deaf and dumb, a great lump of
deaf meat, deaf, deaf, deaf, deaf...

In the cellar I wore dark glasses and switched out
the light, I turned it off and put on the glasses.
I'd seen enough of her to last me a century.

(Pause.)

You heard what I just said.
I'm talking differently now.
Don't think I don't know when that happens.
I'm going to stop talking for good.

INT.   On one wall of the cellar they found Alfonso's
name written up with a piece of coal. Do you
remember writing it?

CLAIRE.   No.

Perhaps I wanted to call him to come and help me?
I couldn't shout.

I have sometimes written to call someone.

INT.   Who?

CLAIRE.   A man who didn't come back.

INT.   On the other wall there was the word 'Cahors'.

CLAIRE.   Really?

INT.   Is it that you can't speak of the cellar or that you
don't want to?

CLAIRE.   I don't want to.

I was just trying desperately to get rid of it. That
was all.

How could I get a corpse weighing twelve stone to
a train? How could I cut a bone without a saw?
They say: 'There was blood in the cellar'. How
can we help there being blood, you and I? I'll
die with my memories of the cellar. I'll take them
with me.

(Pause.)

INT. You intended to go to Cahors?

CLAIRE. Yes. The police were everywhere, in the streets, in the cafes, in the cemeteries, with their dogs. So I said to myself: 'Before they get to the cellars I've got time to go to Cahors for a few days'.

I'd have gone to the Hotel Crystal.

INT. Why didn't you go?

CLAIRE. I called at the Balto. They were talking about the murder. I was interested, and forgot the time. They would keep on saying she'd been killed in the forest.

INT. What did you say to them?

CLAIRE. I said to Alfonso: 'Tell them it was me'. Then he went into the middle of the room and said: 'You needn't look any further, it was Claire Lannes'. At first there was silence. Then shouting.

(Pause during which the interrogator plugs in the tape-recorder. Sound of tape turning and recorded voices.)

PIERRE. She'll be coming back from Cahors, you know, monsieur. Won't you, Claire? You see, she doesn't answer. You have to know her... But she told me...they said goodbye at the door. Claire waited there till the bus went. Tell them, Claire!

CLAIRE. Alfonso! Alfonso!

DETECTIVE. I'm here to take care of you, madame. Don't be frightened. Let's hear what you have to say.

PIERRE. Claire! Claire!

(Pause.)

CLAIRE. She wasn't killed in the forest. It was in a cellar at four o'clock in the morning.

(Silence. Tape stopped. CLAIRE transfixed. They look at each other.)

CLAIRE. Who said that?

INT. Claire Lannes perhaps?

CLAIRE. Perhaps. I recognised the voice. So which of us lied?

135

INT.   Neither. You both told the truth.

CLAIRE.   Oh, then who is lying?

INT.   Pierre Lannes perhaps?

CLAIRE.   Perhaps.

(Pause.)

INT.   What would you have done in Cahors?

CLAIRE.   I'd have walked about the streets. I'd have looked at Cahors.

INT.   But him...the policeman...would you have tried to find him?

CLAIRE.   Perhaps not. What would be the point, now?

Then they would have come for me.

INT.   About the head...

CLAIRE.   Don't start again about the head...

INT.   I want to know in what way it was a problem to you?

CLAIRE.   To know what to do with it. Where to put it. You can't just throw a head on to a train.

I gave it a proper funeral. And I said the prayers for the dead, in spite of the fact that the policeman in Cahors took me away from God.

There, I've ended up saying something about it and I didn't mean to.

INT.   Was it then you realised that you'd killed her?

CLAIRE.   You've guessed?

Yes, it was then. Do you believe me?

INT.   Yes.

CLAIRE.   First of all there was the mark on her neck. When I saw that she started to come back a bit from the dead. Then there was the head. When I saw that she came right back.

They ought to cut my head off too for what I've done. An eye for an eye.

There isn't any grass in the prison yard.

INT.   Soon you'll have another garden.

CLAIRE.   Do you think so?

136

INT. Yes.

CLAIRE. It's sad.

INT. Yes.

CLAIRE. Sometimes I feel mad.

It was a ridiculous life.

INT. You feel mad?

CLAIRE. At night. Yes. I hear things. Sometimes I
believe them.

They beat people to death in cellars. One night
fires started to break out everywhere. The rain put
them out.

INT. Who was beating who?

CLAIRE. The police. The police were beating
foreigners in the cellars of Viorne. Foreigners or
others. They went away when it got light.

INT. Did you see them?

CLAIRE. No. As soon as I came it stopped.

But often I was mistaken. Everything was quiet, quite
quiet and peaceful.

If they search the house don't forget to tell them
there's always been something wrong with the doors
as you come down the stairs.

INT. Who is that for?

CLAIRE. For the women who come after. Is it always
the same with everyone who's done what I've done?

INT. Yes?

CLAIRE. So that's not an explanation?

INT. No. Are you tired now?

CLAIRE. A restful tiredness. Perhaps I'm very close to
being mad. Or dead. Or alive. What do you think?

INT. Alive.

CLAIRE. Ah.

Did I tell you where I put the head?

INT. No.

CLAIRE. Good. I must keep the secret. I talk too much.

No-one ever asked me questions till today. My road led straight to the murder. They ought to keep me shut up.

I'm in with the common law prisoners.

A lawyer came and told me I was going into some home I forget where. I didn't believe him. I behave very well.

I know Alfonso won't come to prison with me. Oh well.

Aren't you going to say anything?

They gave me a pen and paper.

I tried but I couldn't write a word.

And yet I wrote to the papers before, oh often, long letters too. Did I tell you?

INT. In one of them you asked how to keep English mint indoors in winter.

CLAIRE. Did I? I used to eat it sometimes. I wrote a lot of letters. Fifty-three.

Drip drip drip like a drain before the murder. Not so much now.

I'd never have thought it possible.

You don't say anything.

INT. Now you must tell where the head is.

CLAIRE. Was it to get to that question you asked me all the others?

INT. No.

CLAIRE. If the magistrate asked you to ask me that, you can just tell him I didn't answer.

What would you say if I said they're going to put me in the mental hospital at Versailles?

INT. I'd say yes.

CLAIRE. So you're talking to a madwoman?

INT. Yes.

CLAIRE. Why ask me where the head is, then? Perhaps I've forgotten where I put it? Perhaps I can't remember the exact spot?

INT. Just a vague indication would do. One word. Forest. Bank.

CLAIRE. Why?

INT. Just so that you've said it.

CLAIRE. To you?

INT. Yes.

CLAIRE. As a souvenir?

INT. Yes.

(She hesitates.)

CLAIRE. No. Do you hear?

INT. Yes.

CLAIRE. There are other things I haven't told you.

Would you like to know what they are?

INT. No.

CLAIRE. Ah well.

If I told you where the head is would you go on talking to me?

INT. No.

CLAIRE. You've lost heart. Is that it?

INT. Yes.

CLAIRE. If I'd been able to tell you why I killed that big fat deaf woman would you go on talking to me?

INT. No, I don't think so.

CLAIRE. Do you want us to go on trying?

What did I say that suddenly made you lose heart? Is it because time is up?

It's always the same, whether you've done a murder or nothing.

Sometimes my mouth was like the concrete the bench was made of. Did I tell you?

On the ground floor, as you came down the stairs, there were three doors, the first into the dining-room, the second on to the passage, the third her room, they were always open, in a row, and all on the same side, they all tilted the same way, it was as if the whole house sloped in that direction and she'd rolled right past the doors to the bottom, you had to hold on to the banisters.

If I were you I'd listen. Listen.

CURTAIN